A GRIM VOW

Cap poured a dollop of molasses into his tea just like in the old days when dry sugar was hard to find and harder to transport without it going damp and lumpy. He stirred the mixture idly with a twig while his thoughts ranged back in time by a few weeks.

He could as good as see little Rebecca at the dinner table back in Omaha, so childlike and dear. So interested in her grandpap's yarns and so full of a thirst to know and to see all the things he'd talked about.

It had been his fault, Cap felt in some small deep corner of himself, that Rebecca rode the train west with her daddy.

It was his fault the child suffered and died.

His fault. And that of the men who sooner or later would have to answer for the things they'd done to that little girl.

And no one, no one at all, was going to stand in the way of the retribution those men earned when they violated that child.

No one.

Other *Leisure* books by Frank Roderus:
HAYSEED
STILLWATER SMITH

Old Marsden

FRANK RODERUS

LEISURE BOOKS   NEW YORK CITY

A LEISURE BOOK®

April 1999

Published by

Dorchester Publishing Co., Inc.
276 Fifth Avenue
New York, NY 10001

ISBN 0-8439-4506-0

Old Marsden

Chapter One

"Oh, they had me cold, all right. There were eight, maybe ten of them. This was in the autumn of '35, if I remember right. Might've been '34; what year it was didn't matter then and sometimes I wasn't sure just when things were happening. The important thing was taking care of today, not worrying about clocks or calendars or the like. Anyway, me and Billy Hargrew were trapping up on the Musselshell that year. Just the two of us. It was Blackfoot country but Billy was a careful man, and me, back then I figured I'd live forever. Huh! Shows what I didn't know, don't it.

"We'd just moved our camp from one drainage over to the next where we figured the beaver was strong and the pelts likely to be prime. Billy went one way, downstream, and I was going up toward the head of this creek. Oh, I remember it plain as plain can be. I heard the commotion when those red, um, so-an'-so's jumped Billy. They must've had him cold. There was a lot of yelling and he got off one shot, just the one. That was all.

"I knew they were onto us somehow, so I slipped back to camp and threw what gear I could onto our horses. Left Billy's mount there, o' course, just in case he made it, though from the sounds, the fact that there was just the one shot and then the yelling, I didn't figure it was likely he'd show. Still, it wouldn't have done for him to get away an' then be trapped for the lack of a horse, so I left his behind but took what else I could an' headed upcreek with my horse an' the two packhorses. Left most of our gear behind, but then hair is always more important than things. That's something a man learns. Things can be replaced. Blood can't.

"Anyway, I took off fast as I could whilst trying to stay quiet and I thought I'd got away with it. Then I heard a shout from past a thicket of crack-willow and I knew they were onto me. Had me cold or so they thought. I knew there were Injuns following along behind so I couldn't double back. The ones off to my left could see me plain an' were in position to cut me off if I tried to go forward. The only way left was to my right, into this dry cut where the spring melt came down to meet the creek from someplace up above. So of course I turned in there. Turned out to be a short, narrow little gulch. What you might call a box canyon nowadays, although I don't think I'd ever heard that term at the time. For sure those Blackfeet had me trapped cold as a trout caught fresh out of a high mountain stream. Wasn't any way out at the back and them pouring into the mouth of this little gulch. I could see them clear as could be then. Like I said, eight, maybe ten of them. They weren't painted for war. It was just bad luck that put them onto us. They were out hunting or whatever and just stumbled onto us, and that was that.

"Well, I stepped off my old horse and saw to the priming on my rifle and made up my mind that they might could put me under but they wouldn't take me free for nothing. I'd give back as good as I got, and if I made them pay dear enough just mayhap they'd decide one more scalp wasn't worth dying for. With Injuns, see, you never knew. Some days they'd fight long as bulldogs. Other times they'd figure they'd done enough mischief an' just turn and go away. You never knew.

"So there I was, see. Surrounded. Ten Blackfeet out there in the brush and no way past them, and me with only the one bullet in my rifle and a pair of horse pistols to hold them off with. The odds didn't seem what you'd call real good at the time."

He paused, quite consciously drawing out the story, and helped himself to a swallow of coffee that had begun to go cold in the cup during the dissertation.

"What happened next, Grampa?" Both little girls were practically shivering with anticipation. Both had wide eyes fixed firm on the bewhiskered storyteller who sat in an armchair in their comfortable, civilized parlor.

"Do you want me to tell you, Rebecca? I've heard this one before, you see," another voice cut in from the direction of the foyer. A slightly paunchy man wearing a suitcoat, knee-high lace-up boots and a handsomely fashioned necktie stepped into the parlor. "He was surrounded at the back of the box canyon, remember. And of course the Indians killed him." The man threw back his head and roared with laughter.

"Daddy!" one of the girls said in a tone of annoyed disgust. "Really!"

"Sorry, Poppa Marsden. I shouldn't have spoiled your fun. I apologize."

Cap Marsden grunted and smoothed his mustache, then set the coffee cup aside. "That one is an old joke and a good one, George, but in fact the story I'm telling today is true. I really was caught by that bunch of Blackfeet, darn them. And they really did put Billy under that day."

"And you fought your way out past all of them, I take it?" George Brenn challenged.

"No, what I did was I grabbed up what little I could carry, which was mostly my guns and tomahawk and such and, if I remember right, about four of my traps. Left everything else behind for the Blackfeet t' claim whilst I climbed out of that gulch hand over hand. Scampered up the side of that rock wall and took off afoot. The Blackfeet couldn't get atop the cliff in time to see which way I went, and a man on foot don't leave much in the way of tracks for even an Injun to follow. That's why horse stealing parties go out on foot when they raid. Or anyway that's what they used to do. They knew if they got away with horses they could ride clear, but if they were caught they couldn't be tracked back to the home village. Which is beside the point. I left most everything behind and climbed out to get shut of the Injuns, then had to make my way afoot all the way down from Montana to about the middle of Wyoming—or so they are now, back then none of this country had names except what we chose to call one place or another—before I found a band o' friendly Crow where I could get some gear together again. Went to rendezvous that next summer with mighty little to show for a winter's work. But I still had my hair." Cap Marsden pushed a gnarled hand through a thick mop of silver hair and grinned. "Still do if you'll notice."

Which was something of a dig at his son-in-law, for George was already showing signs of baldness even though he was still well short of his fortieth birthday.

"Daddy, please. You've ruined the story. Grampa? Grampā."

"Yes, honey?"

"Tell us about the buffalo. Please."

"Again?"

"Please," the littler of the two pleaded, her eyes large and bright and as pretty as Cap remembered her grandmother's eyes having been. "Please?"

"All right, Cathy. The buffalo . . . haven't I told you about them before now? And haven't you seen them for yourselves? Not ever? Really?"

"Grampa!"

"Oh, all right. The buffalo." Cap took a swallow of the tepid coffee, leaned his chair back on its legs as if it were a rocker, and stared thoughtfully toward the ceiling for a moment while he gathered his thoughts together. For a moment he was distracted. Billy Hargrew. Lordy, he'd been a good partner. Good man too. Cap hadn't thought about Billy in years. And wasn't that a terrible thing. He coughed softly into his fist and tried to concentrate on today. It was already way too late to worry about yesterday and no point in fretting about tomorrow. "Girls," he said after a brief hesitation, "there must be as many buffalo on the plains as there are stars in the heavens. Maybe more. And there isn't any tiny part of them that isn't useful for something. Yes, let me tell you about the buffalo. Now back in the old days . . ."

Chapter Two

Ah, now this was good. Cap felt a glow of contentment flow through his belly, warm and satisfying as a nip of the brandy that he permitted himself—in moderation—now and again. There had been times when it wasn't brandy, but keg alcohol flavored with most anything that came to hand. And no moderation about it either. But that was then and this was now, and this right here was almighty good. For the belly and for the soul. He only wished his Becca—the older grandbaby was named after her, bless them both—had lived to share the moment with him. Becca would have been proud.

Cap and Becca's middle child, Margaret, had married well enough, all things considered. If George Brenn wasn't Cap's idea of perfection, well, Cap wasn't the one as had to live with him. And Lord knew the man doted on his family. He was good to Margaret and to the girls, and he provided for them better than most could've done. They had this fine house in Omaha and a cook to help out in the kitchen and a maidservant to help around the house and serve the meals and such. Most important of all, Margaret seemed happy. That was what counted above all the rest. Their little girl was happy. It did Cap good to see that.

He leaned back in his chair and contemplated the notion of accepting seconds on the dessert. Peach cobbler. Imagine finding fresh peaches all the way out here in the middle of nothing. Well, in the middle of what used to be nothing anyway. It was the railroad that was responsible, of course. With the rails being built, most anything was possible, he supposed. And to think that in a few more years the railroad would span the entire continent, with the Union Pacific building west from this end and some other outfit coming east from California way. Cap marveled to think about it. Why, once those rails got hooked together a train would be able to travel all the way from Omaha clean to the Pacific Ocean. Or so they said, and who was he to doubt it when engineers like George laid the whole plan out on paper and vowed it would be done? Incredible! They said when that happened a man would be able to travel from one ocean to the next in two weeks time. Or less. Incredible indeed. Cap rather hoped he would live long enough to see it all happen. That was a trip he would enjoy taking. Just dang well might do it too if only for the fun of the thing.

Cap's reverie was interrupted, first by the maid offering him another helping of the cobbler—he couldn't turn her down—and then by George. "I have to go to end-of-track next week," Brenn announced. "Would you care to go with me, Poppa Marsden? We're near to South Pass now. How long has it been since you've seen that country?"

"More years than I want to think of," Cap told him. "More years indeed."

"You're welcome to ride along as my guest."

"Will you see buffalo when you go west, Daddy?" Rebecca asked. "Will you?" The child was fourteen now and as pretty as her mother. Little Catherine, at nine, favored Becca more, at least when it came to looks, but Rebecca was her mama's girl, no doubt about that. Rebecca had Margaret's brown hair, a legacy from her grandfather, although his had been white for so long now that she would not recognize where she'd gotten her coloring. It was Cathy who had Becca's fair hair and lively, twinkling eyes.

"Yes, Daddy, will you see buffalo from the cars?" Cathy wanted to know.

"Oh, I suppose so. We most generally do," George admitted without excitement. But then, he saw the huge herds of buffalo frequently. Cap still thought it a pity that the girls never had. Not that there was any hurry. There were so many buffalo on the plains that they would always be there no matter how hard they were hunted by the Indian tribes.

"Can we go too, Daddy?" Rebecca asked.

"Can we?" Cathy echoed.

"Certainly not. End-of-track is not a place for little girls."

"Please?"

"No. I'm sorry, but no." George motioned for the maid to bring coffee. "Now you two excuse yourselves, please, and go up for your baths. Mama and I will be up to tuck you in by and by."

"Daddy!"

"I said no, honey, and I meant it. Go on now. Upstairs. First one in bed gets an extra kiss tonight."

"Grampa, will you talk to him for us? We want to see the buffalo too." Rebecca made a sad, thoroughly pitiful face, which sham Cap did not believe for a moment although he had to admit that her performance was first-rate. "Please, Grampa?"

"Everybody gets to see the buffalo except us," Cathy complained.

"Talk to him, Grampa."

"Upstairs," their father ordered. "Right now."

"Yes, Daddy." Contritely—or so at least they looked—the children excused themselves from the table and went skipping away. Cathy paused at the double doors leading into the dining room. "Will you come up and tell us another story, please, Grampa?"

"Get your baths. I'll come up when you're done."

"A story about the buffalo, Grampa. We want to hear about the buffalo."

Cap gave his son-in-law a mildly apologetic shrug as the little girls thundered up the uncarpeted stairs, sounding quite as loud as one of the buffalo herds that so enthralled them.

"Can we get you something else, Poppa?" Margaret asked.

"No, honey, I couldn't eat another bite." He smiled and patted his belly. "That was wonderful. I only wish . . ." His voice tailed away, the sentence unfinished.

"I know, Poppa. I miss her too."

Cap sighed, trying to hide it from his daughter, and pushed himself away from the table. This was good. Wonderful, really. Now if only Becca could have been here to see it. . . .

Chapter Three

Poor George, Cap thought, not for the first time. The man hadn't a chance. Not with three females squared off against him. When you thought about it, it hardly seemed fair at that. Cap tried to hide a smile as poor George caved in after four days of nearly round-the-clock badgering. "I am telling you," he declared, probably for the last time, "that end-of-track is no place for women or children."

"Oh, pooh, George dear. You told me yourself that Benson Creek has a hotel now. And think about it. All those buffalo. Wild Indians. The great plains. There is so much to see. It will be good for them, for all of us. Why, I've not seen those marvels myself, George. And it will be fun. A vacation. Can't we go with you? All of us?"

"Please." "Please, Daddy." "Please, George dearest."

Brenn, trapped, stricken, his eyes with a haunted, harried look in them, glanced at his father-in-law for support. Cap shrugged. He knew better than to take a minority point of view in this familial dispute. Better to be quiet than to incur the wrath of these three lively ladies whom he loved so dearly. He gave George a pitying glance and then looked away.

"I just don't think it wise," George said lamely.

"Daddy! Really." "Be reasonable, George. Surely your workers are not so rough-and-tumble as all that." "Please, Daddy."

George Brenn coughed into his fist. And abandoned his fight. "All right then. I will wire ahead to make sure there are hotel accommodations for us."

"Thank you, Daddy, thank you!" "Daddy, you're wonderful and I love you!" Margaret merely gave her husband a catlike smile and nodded pleasantly. It was all Cap could do to maintain a straight face. Poor George. He hadn't had a chance. Not from the very beginning.

"This means you only have two days to do your packing," George said with artificial severity. "And mind now, you can't carry everything you own. We will only be there for a few days, and there will not be much in the way of comforts or city amenities. One bag apiece, no more. Do you understand me? One bag each."

"Yes, Daddy." "Of course, dear." "Can I take my dolls, Daddy? Please? Just a few of them?" "Can I ask Letitia to come with us, Daddy?" "Are you sure we can take only one bag for each of us? Really, George. Isn't that taking the notion of roughing it a little far?"

Cap kept a poker face and turned to the sideboard in search of a drink. Poor George. Truly, Cap loved his daughter and grandchildren. But just as truly it was best that his visits happened only once or twice each year.

He poured a generous measure of rye whiskey for

himself—weak stuff it was, nothing at all compared to the popskull they used to brew in the old days—and carried the drink with him onto the front porch, leaving poor George to deal with the ladyfolk on his own.

Cap was a contented man these days. A fortunate man and, perhaps best of all, he knew it. He'd had a fine life. Two good women who'd loved and done for him. First his Crow wife, Sparkling Waters, and then of course Becca. Lucky. And now he had his children. The boys, Alvin Junior, who lived close to Cap's own home back in Santa Fe, and Henry down in Missouri. Both of them had gone into the family business when they were old enough. Both of them were prospering nicely as traders. Margaret here in Omaha with her family. Louise out in San Francisco with her husband and two fine sons. God, Cap was blessed, and he knew it.

It pleased him to think that when George and his railroad completed their work it would be possible for Cap to comfortably and conveniently visit each of his children at least once each year. And who knew, perhaps someday there would even be a railroad connecting Santa Fe with Independence or St. Louis. Cap reminded himself to discuss that likelihood with George. If anyone would know about the possibilities of the future it would be George. Cap gave the man credit for that much anyway. George was bright. He thought ahead. He would know. And if there was a chance that rails might be built along the old Santa Fe Trail it was something that Curry, Marsden and Company should begin thinking about now. Anticipate the coming changes rather than wait and have to react to other people's planning. That was the ticket, Cap told himself. He would talk to George about it first, then to the boys. They should start thinking now about new contracts for freight haulage by rail and an eventual abandonment of the ox wagon trade.

Cap finished his drink and went back inside to pour another, his thoughts whirling ahead to the future. They would want to think about selling off most of their livestock and wagons while there was still a strong market for them. Once a railroad was announced, it would be too late. Then everyone in the business would be wanting to sell off, and there would be a glut on the market. Prices would plummet, and someone was sure to be burned. With a little foresight, Cap thought, he could insure that no harm came to Curry, Marsden and Company.

And in the meantime, why, he could continue to enjoy his retirement . . . well, semiretirement anyway; he supposed he never would completely divorce himself from productive activity. Not so long as his health and acuity of mind held.

And really, for a man edging into his sixties, Alvin Douglas Marsden was in excellent shape, lean and fit if not quite so spry as once he'd been. He could still sit a horse from can-see to can't-see, could still hold a steady aim—as more than a few competitors at Santa Fe's Rifle and Gun Club would unhappily attest—could still hold his whiskey and his water, could still . . . um, best not to be thinking about that. Not here in Omaha where word of dalliance might get back to Margaret or the grandchildren. Could still at any rate hold his own as a man among men in most all the ways that genuinely counted. And for all of that Cap Marsden was most truly grateful.

He took a final swallow of the rye, which really was flavorsome, albeit weak, and went back inside to see how George was holding up in the face of the excitement he'd caused.

Frank Roderus

This trip promised to be an interesting one, Cap thought. And it really would be nice to see the South Pass country again. God, how many years had it been? He tried to think back. . . .

Chapter Four

He came awake instantly, with no moment of hesitation or befuddlement to mark the transition from sleep to alert interest. He'd heard . . . what? Something. A threat? No, not here. Not in his daughter's house in Omaha. But something was amiss. He knew that.

Sure of his movements even in the dark, Cap stood, his nightshirt falling to tickle the backs of his calves, and made his way to the door leading into the hall. He could see light at the transom and beneath the door. At this late hour the place should have been in darkness.

Barefoot, Cap stepped out into the hallway to listen. He cold hear whispering from somewhere off to his left, from the direction of the bedroom shared by the children. Their door opened and Margaret's housemaid slipped out carrying a basin.

"Is something wrong, Brenda?" His voice, not particularly loud, startled her and she had to take care to avoid spilling whatever it was she had in the basin. A moment longer and the sharply acid stink of vomit told Cap why the young maid did not want to cause a spill that would add to her work. "Who's sick?" Cap asked.

"The little one," the housemaid told him. "Miss Catherine."

Cap padded down the hall to peek inside. Margaret was there leaning over Cathy's bed. Rebecca was sitting up in her own bed, giving her sister a look that mingled sisterly concern with sisterly annoyance.

"Is everything all right?" Cap asked from the doorway. Cathy did not appear all right. Not in the least. She was pale, her eyes huge in the light of a single lamp and wet with tears. "What is it, honey?"

"Her stomach is upset and I think she has a fever," Margaret responded.

"Nothing serious, I hope."

"Probably not, but I'll not take any chances. We won't be able to go with you and George tomorrow. I'll keep the girls here with me. You two gentlemen can go see the sights by yourselves. We ladies," she ran a hand over Cathy's brow, but the gesture did nothing to ease the hurt of disappointment that Cap could see in the little girl's eyes, "we ladies will have to wait until next time."

"Mama, that isn't fair," Rebecca protested. "I'm not sick. Why can't I go with Daddy and Grampa? Just because Cathy can't go doesn't mean I should have to miss seeing the buffalo and the wild Indians and everything."

"Not now, dear. We will talk about this in the morning. Poppa, would you hand me that cloth, please? And the water pitcher? I want to see if I can bring this fever down a little so she can sleep. She feels awfully warm to me."

Cap fetched the articles as requested and reached

a leathery, much-weathered hand down to touch his granddaughter's forehead. She did indeed seem to have a fever. A fairly high one at that. Margaret dampened the cloth, wrung it nearly dry, and gently patted Cathy's cheeks and forehead and used the cooling water to bathe the child's throat and chest as well.

"Grampa, don't let Mama keep me here. I want to go too. I'll be fine in the morning. Really," the little girl appealed.

"We'll all do what your parents decide, sweetheart," Cap told her.

"Grampa—"

"You too, Rebecca. Your mom and daddy know best."

"But I'm not at all sick. I shouldn't have to stay at home and miss all the fun just because Cathy is. It isn't *fair*." Rebecca's voice became shrill and whiny.

"That will be quite enough of that, young lady," Margaret declared, but it was clear that her concern right now was directed toward Cathy, and so there was no particular conviction in the words. "Please be quiet now. Poppa, would you please go see what is keeping Brenda downstairs?"

"What is it you want, dear?"

"I want to give her some spirits of ammonia. A spoonful in a glass of water. And I need a hot poultice to put on her stomach."

"I'll go see what I can do," Cap told his daughter. Cap turned and made his way through the mostly darkened house, a lean and wiry old man with sleep-tousled hair and a rumpled nightshirt. This promised, he thought, to be a long night yet. He doubted that any of them would feel much like traveling tomorrow. Well, except for George, that is. Margaret's husband seemed capable of sleeping through nearly anything, and this upset with the children was no exception. George would likely feel fit as a fiddle come daybreak, but Cap was not so sure about the rest of them.

Chapter Five

Poor George, Cap thought. He hadn't any idea how often in the past he'd reached that same conclusion. Plenty, that was for sure. The thing was, the poor fellow was just plain out of his depth when it came to dealing with women. George simply did not know how to handle them. Why, he really expected females to reason with him. Cap himself had long ago concluded that the only way to deal with women was to lay down the law and then ignore any pleas or protests that might arise. And he'd stuck with that too. Except occasionally, that is.

In any event, he told himself, he would not have allowed a fourteen-year-old like Rebecca, sweet granddaughter though she was, to decide for herself that she was going along on the trip west even though Cathy was sick and their mother would have to remain behind in Omaha to tend to the younger child.

Poor George, though, had given in to Rebecca's wheedling and now had her baggage right there beside her father's, ready to be taken to the depot and loaded onto the Union Pacific private car that carried important company officials and distinguished visitors. That car was said to be something of a marvel itself. It was something Cap thought he likely would enjoy seeing. But not today.

"You're sure you won't change your mind and go with us, Poppa Marsden?" George asked. "It isn't too late, you know."

"Thank you, George, but I think it will be best if I stay here. Margaret may need help with Cathy, and I wouldn't feel right about leaving them alone. I'll go with you the next time."

Rebecca made a pouty face, which Cap ignored completely. "It would be ever so much more fun with you along, Grampa. You could tell us your stories and what it used to be like in the western country."

"Next time, sweetheart. That's a promise."

"Please?"

Cap did not bother to answer, but picked up Rebecca's bags and carried them to the street, where a Union Pacific coach had just pulled up ready to transport the family to the depot. It occurred to Cap that George probably was a rather important man and most likely a capable one in his own element. Certainly he made a very good living for Margaret and the children. Cap was thankful for that. But then all of his children had turned out well, even seemed to be happy with themselves and their lives. Margaret was not an exception. One of many blessings that Cap could count, he supposed.

Margaret rushed outside at the last minute to give Rebecca a kiss good-bye and deliver a hug to her husband, never mind that they were right there in public. Cap felt a rush of warmth into his cheeks at the public display of affection. This modern generation seemed quite different from his own.

Cap gave Rebecca a light buss on the top of her head and a handshake to George and a moment later the coach pulled away.

"They'll be just fine," Cap assured his daughter as, one arm around her shoulders, he walked her back inside.

"Rebecca has never been away from me, Poppa. It scares me a little."

"Of course it does, dear, but she'll be just fine. George will see to that. And right now we have to concern ourselves with Cathy. Is she feeling any better this morning?"

"She says she feels fine now. She wants to grab her things and go along with Rebecca and her daddy."

Cap laughed. "Sounds like what you would have claimed a few years ago, even if you'd been so sick you couldn't stand up."

"Oh, Poppa. I was never like that."

"Of course you were. You just don't want to remember it like that, but you were. Trust me."

Margaret gave him a skeptical look and changed the subject. "Would you go upstairs and talk with Cathy, Poppa? Tell her some more of your stories, please? I think she would like that."

"You know it doesn't take much encouragement to get me to talking about the old times." He waited until they were indoors, then gave Margaret a light kiss on the cheek. "Brenda and I will see to whatever Cathy needs for a spell, dear. Why don't you take a nap? You were up the whole night long. You must be exhausted."

"I don't think I could sleep now anyway, Poppa. I'm worried about Rebecca, to say nothing of Cathy being so sick."

27

"Don't fret yourself, dear. Rebecca will be fine." He smiled. "You'll see."

The telegraphic message giving lie to that prophecy arrived two days later.

Chapter Six

"How is Margaret holding up?" George asked before Cap so much as had a chance to set foot on the makeshift platform at the Benson Creek railroad depot.

"Not good. But then what can you expect," Cap returned. "I almost had to lock her in to keep her from coming."

"Cathy?"

"She's still sick. That's the only reason I was able to convince Margaret she should stay at home. Which will be the best thing for her anyway. The news is sure to be bad enough. Margaret shouldn't have to see for herself. Just knowing will be all she'll be able to bear."

George did not seem to understand what Cap was saying. Which probably was just as well, Cap decided. The telegram indicated that George Brenn still had some illusions. Cap did not. He knew good and well what they could expect to find, even if George didn't. "Your message didn't tell us all that

29

much, George. Go over it for me, please."

The distraught father wrung his hands. He was pale and nervous and obviously frightened. He spent a few moments collecting his thoughts before he answered. "We were in the hotel, of course, the same as we'd planned all along. Adjoining rooms. I saw Rebecca into bed about, I think, nine o'clock. Tucked her in, then went in and read over the surveyor's reports before I went to bed myself. I didn't hear her get up and go outside. Nothing like that. I never heard a sound from her. In the morning her room was just . . . empty."

"The bed had been slept in?"

"Yes, she'd been to bed all right. I tucked her under the covers that evening, remember."

"But did the sheet and pillow look rumpled? Or more fresh than you would have expected?"

"I . . . can't say that I paid any particular mind to that," George answered.

"No one saw her after you put her to bed? No one else heard anything?"

"No one. Believe me, we've asked."

"*We?*" Cap repeated. "There's a lawman here?"

"Not really. No one official, if that's what you mean. By *we* I mean myself and the railroad bosses. If there is any authority in town I suppose we would have to be considered it, at least until a government is organized. None has been so far. But everyone here has been cooperative. The townspeople are rough, sure, but no one would countenance anyone doing harm to a child nor to a decent woman. That simply would not be tolerated."

"Uh-huh. What about the hotel? Was there a clerk on duty all night?"

"The rooms were all taken. He closed the front door about ten, he said, and lay down on a cot in the office. He didn't see or hear anyone either.

There's a bell set over the front door. It rings whenever the door is opened. But the man can't swear that he would have heard if anyone came in after he fell asleep."

"What about the chamber pot in Rebecca's room?" Cap asked. "Was it used?"

"I . . . don't know."

"Has the room been cleaned since Rebecca disappeared?"

"I suppose so. I can ask. Is that important?"

Cap shrugged. The truth, of course, was that he didn't know what was important. Or what was not. "We'll ask," he said. "I presume you've looked for her?"

"Of course. The whole town has. I think they've barged into every shop, house, shed, or shanty anywhere close by. The railroad pulled two crews away from unloading the flatcars and had them search too. They couldn't find anything. There was . . . nothing, I'm afraid."

"Never mind what you know for the moment, George. What do you think might have happened?"

"Rebecca wouldn't have gone out at night. Not onto the street, I mean. She isn't that unruly a child. Not to say that she isn't adventuresome, but she's not a foolish girl. She would not have gone out like that. What I think is that sometime during the night she had to relieve herself. And she isn't accustomed to using a chamber pot, you see. We have the water closet at home. She's used to having things . . . more comfortable than they are here. I think she probably went outside. To the privy, I mean. And . . ." He shook his head. "I don't know after that. I can't begin to guess."

Cap could. But he did not think it a good idea to offer suggestions. Not to George. Certainly not right now. "Is there any likelihood Rebecca might have run off of her own accord? To see wild Indians or whatever?"

"No, of course not. She saw some of those pathetic blanket Indians in Cheyenne. She was frightened of them. I'm sure she wouldn't have run away so she could see any more of them close up. Why, she wouldn't get out of the cars in Cheyenne for fear one of them might grab her." George's face twisted. "Oh God. Why did I let her come out here? Why didn't I insist she stay safe at home?"

"Is anyone missing?" Cap asked.

George gave him an uncomprehending stare.

"Other than Rebecca, I mean. Is there anyone not in town who normally would be here? Have any men disappeared too?"

"I don't think so. I'm not sure."

"What about people passing through? Hotel guests, for instance?"

"There were two parties registered at the hotel that night other than railroad personnel. I suppose they went on about their business."

"They're not still in town? Neither group?"

"No, I don't think so."

"How many men? Who were they?"

"We can ask at the desk."

"The hotel will tell us?"

"Oh, yes. I guarantee it."

"You're still searching, I hope."

"Of course. The railroad sent word to the advance parties calling in our meat hunters and a tracker. They should get back sometime this afternoon or tonight."

"Why is it taking so long?" Cap asked.

They were in territory that George knew and understood now, and his answer was firm. "You have to understand, Poppa Marsden, that end-of-track is not so much one place as a succession of them. A process, you might even say. Right now we are at the most advanced supply point. But the actual track-laying is some miles west of here. The tie crews are working ahead of that and the road graders in advance of them. The surveyors are working probably thirty or more miles ahead of the grading gangs, and the scouts and hunting parties are west of them. End-of-track, such as it is, runs fifty or more miles depending on what you care to think of as being a part of it. It isn't just this one little place. And when we move our supply point forward, Benson Creek may well dry up and disappear. Or it may continue a quieter existence than it has now. Most of the towns flourish for a few weeks or a month, then go under. Take a look at the buildings you see here. Notice anything odd? There are no foundations. Most of the buildings are on skids. When end-of-track moves, so will they. Even the hotel. The owners will hitch ox teams to the structures and drag them ahead to the next camp. I doubt Benson Creek will exist a month from today."

"I had no idea."

"Of course not. You aren't Union Pacific," George said, a tinge of pride in his voice. Then, as he remembered, the man's face crumpled in sorrow. "Not that that will matter," he whispered. "Oh, God. We have to find her. We have to."

"We will, George. I promise you that. We'll find your little girl."

"I wish I could believe that, Poppa Marsden. God knows I wish I could believe you."

"Come along, George. I want to talk to the people at the hotel."

Chapter Seven

The hotel clerk, a man named Bryan, although whether that was his first name or last Cap never did decide, appeared almost as concerned as George was. He also proved to be more helpful.

"There were the two parties registered the night the young lady disappeared," Bryan said. "A party of four traveling east from Salt Lake. On business, they said. In Indiana, if I remember correctly. I assumed they were saints."

Cap raised an eyebrow, skepticism plain in his expression.

"I didn't mean that sort of saint, sir. I mean, I'm not attempting to speak to their character. What I meant was that I assumed them to be part of the Mormon faith. Saints. That's what they call themselves."

"I see," Cap said, not at all sure that he did. He'd heard about the Mormon faith, some sort of radical religious movement that had settled the land around the salt-laden lake in what was now called

Desert or sometimes Utah. Cap himself was years gone from this part of the country by the time the Mormons came, however, and he knew little about them. He supposed anyone who thought of themselves as being saints could not be all bad. Nor fully in touch with reality, for that matter. "You say they were headed east?"

"Yes, I'm sure about that. They asked how they would go about getting rail transport eastward. I told them as best I could."

"Do you know if they went?"

"They said they were on the way to the U.P. office when they checked out come morning. I would assume they caught the next available coach headed that way."

"I can check that easily enough, Poppa Marsden," George volunteered.

"Please. You did see these men in the morning, then?" Cap asked of the hotel clerk.

"Oh, yes. They had breakfast here and recovered some boxes I'd stored for them in the office."

"And they were alone?"

"If you mean was young Miss Brenn with them, certainly not. There were only the four of them, same as when they checked in the night before. If you want their names, I have them on the guest register."

"And the second party?"

"Three men."

"Eastbound also?"

"They never said."

"Saints?"

"I wouldn't know, but I doubt it. The Mormons don't hold much with hard liquor, most of them. There's some will get rowdy once they get off the reservation, so to speak, but mostly they tend to act the same as they talk, and they generally oppose spirits. This bunch I'm telling you about, they liked their whiskey. I could smell it on them when they came in. Not that it's any of my business what a man cares to do, of course. It isn't like they were causing trouble. They weren't. They went to the room I gave them, then came out later and went out somewhere. I wouldn't know where. I never saw them again after that."

"What about in the morning?" Cap asked. "You didn't see them again then?"

"No, they were already gone by the time I opened up again."

"Is that unusual?"

"Not particularly. Folks come and go. They don't have to account for what they want to do."

"Do you know if these men were horseback or if they came in by coach?"

"I have no idea."

"I assume the first group, the four men . . . ?"

"Yes?"

"I assume the four travelers would've gotten here by coach if they were looking for transportation east?"

"That makes sense," Bryan agreed. "They must have."

"Did the party of three check in about the same time of day? Like if they'd all arrived on the same coach, I mean?"

"No, the three got here later on in the evening. Though I suppose they could've arrived on the stage and spent some time in a saloon before hiring the room. Like I said, I'm sure they'd all had something to drink."

"What about their luggage?"

"Um, carpetbags."

"No bedrolls?"

"No, but if they had horses they could have left

their beds with the rest of their gear, wherever they put the horses up overnight."

"I can find out if they used the company corrals," George offered.

"Good. And you say you never saw them again after they went out that evening? You didn't see them in the morning?"

"That's right. But like I told you, it isn't particularly unusual. A good many travelers like to get an early start."

"Was there a train leaving overnight?" Cap asked.

"I can answer that one, Poppa Marsden. We had nothing running that night. Not in, not out."

"So they had their own transportation," Cap mused.

Bryan shrugged.

"Tell me what the three looked like."

"You think they would know something about Miss Brenn?" Bryan asked.

"Who else?" Cap returned. "It pretty much has to be them."

"I'll tell you everything I can remember about them."

"And their names? Did they sign the register too?"

The clerk brought out a canvas-bound ledger, but the entry for that date showed only a scrawled X mark where the name of the man hiring the room should have been. It was not at all unusual. Roughly a third of the transients who registered in the book signed similarly.

"When did you say these hunters and trackers of yours should be here, George?"

Chapter Eight

Poor George—Cap could not help thinking of his son-in-law that way, it seemed—was beside himself with the delay. The trackers would not arrive until late afternoon and could not be expected to start after the threesome until dawn at the earliest.

"I don't see how you can be so calm, Poppa Marsden," George said at one point early in the afternoon.

Cap shook his head sympathetically but knew better than to explain. There was no hurry. Not now, he was sure. Rebecca was already dead. If those men took her—and he had to believe that surely they must have—once they sobered up in the harsh glare of day, they would know they could not afford to be found with a kidnapped white girl. An Indian child they could certainly get away with. Even a Negro or Mexican perhaps. But a white girl? That was a sure and certain path to a hanging.

No, if the three had been stupid enough, impulsive enough to kidnap Rebecca to begin with, by now they surely would have murdered her and tried to hide her body. Cap knew that. George obviously did not. Poor George even sent a wire to Margaret back home in Omaha telling her they had a lead on the kidnappers and should soon be on their trail. Cap wished George hadn't done that. False hope was worse than no hope at all in his mind. And any hopes George raised were sure to be false ones.

"Try to get some rest while you're waiting, George," Cap advised. "You aren't used to hard riding."

"What about you?"

"I have some purchases to make this afternoon," Cap told him.

"I've already arranged horses and camping equipment for both of us, Poppa Marsden."

"Yes, I recall. Thank you."

"Is there anything . . . ?"

"Nothing you can do, George. Thank you. Go on now. Lie down. Rest while you can. Tomorrow will be a hard day."

Cap doubted poor George would take the advice, but it was well-intended and probably sound. It was up to George what he chose to do, however.

Cap left the hotel and, following directions given by the hotel man Bryan, found what passed for a hardware store in Benson Creek.

"Yes, sir," the clerk responded to Cap's question. "I have the best selection this side of Omaha, sir. Almost sold out, though. You got here just in time."

"Oh, how's that?"

"The manhunt. Surely you've heard. There's a manhunt going out first thing come morning. Practically every man jack in the vicinity will be along. A white girl was kidnapped, or so they say. Terrible thing, of course. But good for business. I'm 'most sold out of revolving pistols and prepared cartridges." The man leaned forward and lowered his voice a notch in feigned confidentiality. "And of rope. 'Most sold out of strong hemp too, d'you see?"

Cap scowled. Not at the thought of a hanging. If it were to happen, that would be no more than justice. No, what he objected to was the idea that every idiot at end-of-track with the ability to find a horse and a gun would be joining the procession come tomorrow morning.

The manhunt was more apt to turn into a circus than a tracking party. Worse, they would probably destroy more sign than even the best of trackers could ever hope to find.

And that Cap would not, could not, countenance. To the men here, this hunt would be as much a lark as a serious effort to exact justice for whatever crimes were committed against Cap's naive and trusting granddaughter.

Cap's own intentions were serious in the extreme.

"Show me what you have left," he said.

"Revolvers, sir?"

"No short guns, thank you. Can't say as I understand those things very much. Something with some punch to it."

"I have some old Springfield muskets. Very cheap and not too badly worn."

"No, I'll be wanting the best you have," Cap said. "Don't worry. I can pay for what I want."

The clerk looked at him again, a thin and wiry old man with graying hair and sun-weathered skin. "Whatever you say, sir. I, uh, have you heard of the new Winchester model?"

"Shoots the same .44 rimfire as the Henry but without the split in the loading tube?"

"You have heard of it. Good. I, um, have one of those put by. I could let you have it for, say, fifty dollars?"

"List price is twenty-seven," Cap told him.

"Yes, it is. You can buy one for that in 'most any hardware or gunsmith's in Omaha, I should think."

"I'll take it for the fifty. And shells to go with it. Three boxes should do." Cap wished he had his own custom Scheutzen long-range target rifle, but the big gun built on a Sharps falling block action was back home in Santa Fe and of no use now that he needed it here. "And I'll be wanting a pair of knives. Let me see what you have to choose from. A trade tomahawk, plain iron, nothing fancy. Flat file, very fine grain. Whetstone, the best Arkansas you've got. And let me think what else. . . ."

The store clerk began to look like a very happy man at the prospect of his profit from this sale.

Chapter Nine

Circus, he'd said? Lord, he reckoned. It was a circus and worse. Bunch of hungover young fools with big pistols and bigger mouths on them. There were— he counted—twenty-three of them, not counting him and George. About half of them looked like they would fall out of their saddles if the borrowed horses stumbled. And as for tracking down a bunch of kidnappers, well, Cap had his doubts and then some.

"They don't look like much, Poppa Marsden," George said, echoing Cap's opinion, albeit couched in a watered-down and somewhat more charitable form of speech. "But don't be put off by what you see here. These are all good men, combat veterans of the war, every one of them. They'll come through. You'll see."

Cap offered no response to that optimistic assessment. He squinted toward the east, where the morning sun was all too soon to break the horizon. There was more than enough light to start off by, so why were they milling around here like so many lost sheep?

"Ah, good," George mumbled. "Here comes Cactus Bob. We'll be able to begin now."

Cap looked in the direction George indicated. Cactus Bob. Lordy, what a name. Probably conferred upon himself, Cap decided grumpily. Cactus Bob. Huh! The man was just as impressive as all billy hell to look at. Had long blond hair falling in curls beneath a coyote-skin cap, a brace of huge revolving pistols carried in a scarlet sash at his waist—none too small a waist, Cap noticed; the man would be fat as a Missouri hog before he was forty—and a set of fancy Mexican spurs big enough to nearly drag the ground . . . and that was when he was horseback. There was no telling how he would manage to walk in those silly, ineffective, show-up things.

The man rode direct to George and touched the little leather half-moon brim that was grafted onto the front of the dead coyote perched on his head. He looked, Cap thought, like he was posing for a portrait.

"Good morning, Mr. Brenn." He bobbed his head obsequiously to George, then looked at Cap and his eyebrows went up. "And you, sir, would be . . . ?"

"This is my father-in-law," George told him.

"Oh. Of course. You, uh, think you will be able to keep up, sir?"

"I'll do my best," Cap told the man, his voice dry as summer in Santa Fe.

"Captain Marsden is familiar with the country here, Cactus Bob. You may wish to call upon him for advice."

"Certainly," Cactus Bob (Cap wondered if the young fool had a family name . . . or if maybe no one wanted to claim him) said in a voice so serious it was clear he had no intention whatsoever of seeking advice from an old codger like this one. "Captain, you said."

"Not in your war," Cap put in quickly.

"I see," Cactus Bob said, although he obviously did not. Cactus Bob did not ask for a further explanation, and Cap did not choose to offer one either. "Don't let us hold you up, sonny. We'd best be about this. The men have a three-day start on us as it is."

"Right," Cactus Bob said crisply, wheeling his horse and cantering to the front of the pack of armed lunatics who were responsible for hunting down the three men who'd kidnapped Rebecca.

At least the man managed to sit a horse, Cap reluctantly conceded. Didn't fall off and looked good. Which Cactus Bob obviously knew.

"Cactus Bob is our chief scout and hunter," George explained. "Quite a colorful sort, don't you think?"

"He is that," Cap said slowly, not wishing to burst George's bubble with any elaboration. "Where's he from?"

"Oh, he's a westerner through and through. From Iowa, I believe. Dubuque."

"Uh-huh." Cap was of the impression that there weren't a lot of plains Indians around that end of Iowa. But then what did he know? He'd never been there.

"He's a good man. Recommended to us by Buffalo Bill Cody and Texas Jack Omohundro."

"Uh-huh," Cap grunted again. And since no opinion had been sought, none was offered.

"Listen up, men," Cactus Bob was shouting at the noisy, uncoordinated crowd of riders who comprised the manhunt. "You all know the situation. It is our privilege to hunt down the three men who kidnapped Rebecca Brenn. We will find them. We

44

will rescue Mr. Brenn's little girl. And we will bring these men back here, where proper justice can be administered."

That brought a sort of roaring growl from the men, at least some of whom must have been awake and aware enough to listen.

"Martin, Drayton, Collier," Cactus Bob called. "You three out front, if you please. I want you to spread out on point. You know what to look for. When you find sign, signal the main body. We will follow close behind. And every man of you, see to your weapons. We have to assume that these men will fight if cornered, that they will run if pursued. It is our job to see that they do not escape justice. Now." He stood in his stirrups and paused dramatically while sweeping off his coyote cap and glaring magnificently into the distance toward nothing in particular. "Are you with me?"

"YAR!" The deep, throaty roar was immediate, rising from at least a score of voices.

"Right." Cactus Bob wheeled his horse, spurring it and drawing back on his reins at the same time, so the animal's front feet came off the ground as it pawed the air before it. "Point riders, deploy. Men, follow me."

Maybe, Cap thought, just maybe he'd underestimated this Cactus Bob whoever-he-was.

Cap darn well hoped so, anyway.

The point riders cantered north away from end-of-track while the crowd of milling horsemen sorted themselves into no particular order and followed at a slower pace, with Cactus Bob leading the pack.

Cap and George Brenn trailed well behind the others, George looking impatient but too innately polite to abandon his father-in-law, and Cap unwilling—he did not explain it to George—to ride in the cloud of choking dust churned up by the hoofs of the two dozen horses in front of them.

After all, there was no hurry about any of this. Not now.

Chapter Ten

Had he said this outfit was a circus? That hadn't been the half of it, Cap decided, based on several hours of observation. The whole deal was a circus, and Cactus Bob was the head clown. Except a clown at least knew how to make folks laugh. Cap was not laughing about what he saw now.

At noon—at an alkali-laced water hole that wasn't fit for man nor beast even though there was sweet water not two miles distant, as any man could have figured out if he only knew to pay attention to game trails on the ground and bird movements in the air—Cap wandered over to where Cactus Bob was holding forth over a cup of coffee.

"Know this country, do you?" he asked, his expression a study in innocence.

"Old man, I've hunted this country one end to the other for the past three, four years. There's hardly a deer in the woods that I don't know on a first-name basis," Cactus Bob informed him.

"That so, eh? And where do you figure those men are bound?"

"The Idaho gold fields," Cactus Bob said firmly.

"Sure of that, are you?"

"It's what one of them said in the saloon the other night," Cactus Bob explained.

"You talked to them?"

"Not me. Harry Blair over there. He remembers them."

"And they said they're bound for Idaho?"

"That's right. For the new gold diggings at a place they call Virginia City. Up at the north end of the Bozeman Trail, that's where."

"I hadn't heard that. Is, uh, is this here the Bozeman?"

"Not hardly. That's over east a way. But it angles toward the west. I figure them to run straight north. Meet up with the wagon trail somewhere east of Virginia City and follow it on in."

"And you believe you can just ride north to find the men and this Bozeman road?"

"That's right. It won't be no problem."

Cap wondered if he should bring up minor details like the Wind River mountains. Or the terrifyingly deep canyons. Or the wildly colored stinking springs that lay to the north, between this barren near-desert where they now traveled and the green hills where they were said to have found gold. He doubted Cactus Bob had any inkling what lay between him and the Bozeman. Cap had spent the better part of twenty years wading the beaver streams in this country before he went south to settle in Santa Fe. He doubted that anyone who knew the land would choose the route Cactus Bob intended to follow.

"I don't suppose your trackers are following actual sign of the men," Cap ventured.

"You got to understand, old man, that it isn't that easy. They've picked up some horse prints, proba-

48

bly from the men we want. But they have a long lead on us. Right now we want to make up time, close in on them, like. We'll start finding tracks to follow as we get closer."

"Uh-huh," Cap said politely. "Are your people looking for my granddaughter's body when they ride? Are they looking for anything like that?"

"We're gonna bring that little girl back safe and sound, mister," Cactus Bob declared. "And that's a promise."

"You, sir, are a fool," Cap said in a deceptively soft level voice. "Rebecca wouldn't have survived half a dozen hours once those three sobered up enough to realize what they'd done when they took her."

"We didn't ride out here to find a body, old man. We came to save a child."

"Then I'll say it again, sir. You are a fool."

Cactus Bob came to his feet, fists balled and quick anger making a red, glowering mask of his face. He stood quivering but held himself back. The self-control, Cap knew good and well, had nothing to do with fear. Likely it was concern about his future with the railroad that kept Cactus Bob from walloping George Brenn's father-in-law. Whatever the reason, Cap did not contest it. He had no desire to hurt this young dandy who thought so much of himself.

Cap returned to George's side and began tightening the cinches on the horse George had found for him.

"Going somewhere, Poppa Marsden?"

"Uh-huh. These boys mean well, but they'll never find Rebecca or the men that took her. I will."

"I can't believe—"

"You do what you want, George. Do whatever you think best."

"You're going on alone?"

"Going back alone. I'll start from the beginning and see what I can find."

"We're half a day on the trail, Poppa Marsden."

"Uh-huh. Wrong trail." Cap took a tin coffee cup, dumped the grounds from it, and tied it to a string behind his cantle. That, along with a blanket already tied in place there and the few items he carried on his person, constituted all the equipment he believed necessary.

"Wait, I . . . give me a few minutes to talk with Cactus Bob," George said. "I can't let you go off alone, dammit."

Cap didn't know whyever not. But if George wanted to come, he was entitled. After all, it was his daughter who'd been taken. "I'll wait for you here," was all he said.

He did not want to overhear whatever explanations George offered for the defection. Probably George was merely humoring Margaret's father. Probably George would say exactly that to the Union Pacific employees who were participating in the official search.

That was just fine. Cap did not much give a damn how George wanted to explain it so that feathers would not be ruffled nor feelings hurt.

Cap merely wanted to get about the business of doing what had to be done here.

Business that had to do not with rescue but with revenge.

A man does not, after all, allow his own to be violated without retribution.

Chapter Eleven

They were within sight of the columns of smoke rising from dozens of supper fires marking the not quite visible end-of-track before Cap decided they were far enough south to begin his search for the men who'd taken Rebecca.

"We'll be heading east now," he told George, who for the past several hours had been growing increasingly nervous as Cap's path took them farther and farther away from what George obviously regarded as the "real" search party.

"Why?" George grumbled.

"Because that's where we'll find their trail, of course."

"You know that for a fact, do you?"

"George, if you want to go back and join up with Cactus Bob and those other drunks, go right ahead."

"I only asked a question, Poppa Marsden. I thought it a reasonable enough one under the circumstances."

Cap thought about that for a moment, then nodded. "Yes, I suppose it is. All right. We'll turn east here because the men will have ridden northeast once they left the hotel."

"How can you know that?"

"That fellow they spoke with in the saloon before they took Rebecca—"

"How do you know it was before they took her, Poppa Marsden?"

"These are evil men we're after, George. I know that because they took the girl. But that isn't to say they're stupid men. They know good and well they did something they can't allow anyone else to know. They have to hide what they did. So as soon as they took her—and God knows how that came about; probably they were all visiting the outhouse at the same time or something that ordinary—whatever the truth of that, just as soon as they took her they will have known they had to hide the fact. Had to get away from civilized folk and out into the brush where they could do whatever they wanted without being heard or seen. So they would have packed up their gear and headed out right then and there. Maybe sent one or two inside to get their bedrolls while at least one of them held onto Rebecca either at the place where they left their horses or somewhere outside of town where the others could easily pick them up on the way out. And then they would have ridden north and east."

"But—"

"I know that, George, because the Idaho gold fields—Montana some are calling that country now, I hear—those gold camps are where they're bound. That's what they said in the saloon and there's no reason to think they changed their minds after."

"What if they were moving west to begin with?"

"Not with Idaho in mind for a destination, they weren't. If they'd wanted to go to Virginia City from anywhere east of here they would have gone through Cheyenne, not end-of-track. It wouldn't make sense otherwise, for the Bozeman Trail runs east of the Big Horns. In order to reach the Bozeman from here they have to have been coming from the west, the Mormon country or California or wherever, and they have to be heading east to get south of the Big Horns and pick up the wagon road."

"Cactus Bob thinks they will have gone straight north, not turned east from here."

"Cactus Bob is an idiot," Cap said succinctly. "He doesn't know the first thing about the country that lies between here and Virginia City. No, if those men know enough to be traveling cross-country at all, they know enough to go east of the Big Horns. That's where they'll be heading."

"And if they don't know any more than you say Cactus Bob does? If they do ride north?"

"Then Cactus Bob and his friends will find them after all, and I'll be proved wrong. I been wrong about things before, George. I won't mind it happening again if it means those men are brought back and hanged. But George, I won't take any chance at all that they might ride away from this unpunished. That I simply will not countenance."

George looked at him, a gray-haired old man slouched in the saddle of a borrowed horse with a rifle laid across his pommel. Not even carried in a saddle scabbard like any sensible man would do, but held in his hand the whole while he rode, the way an Indian might do, not a white man. George grunted, but kept silent about whatever further questions or comments he might have wanted to make.

"You ready to move along, George?"

"Whenever you say, Poppa Marsden."

Chapter Twelve

"Damn," Cap muttered under his breath. He was not generally given to strong language, considered it a weak man who thought he had to resort to that kind of talk in order to appear strong, but . . . this was different.

He'd been expecting this for the past day and a half, ever since they turned away from what passed for civilization back there along the railroad right of way. Expecting it, yes. That did not mean it was something he'd wanted to find.

"Damn," he repeated softly to himself.

"Did you say something, Poppa Marsden?"

"No, George. I tell you what, George. Do you see that rock formation over there? The one with the brush growing just to the left of it?"

"I do."

"I want you to keep on toward it. If I haven't caught up with you by the time you get there, stop and make our noon fire. There's a seep of sweet water just above those rocks if I remember right.

Make our fire and wait for me, will you?"

George gave his father-in-law a bluntly skeptical look. "You're sure?"

"George, it's been, what? Thirty years? Thirty-five? No, I'm not sure about the water. But I'm sure we can noon there. Just wait for me, all right?"

"Fine, whatever you say." George continued forward at the same plodding, dogged pace Cap had maintained from the beginning. The gait was not swift, but the horses were always fresh and there was seldom any need to stop and rest them.

Cap reined his own mount to the east, well off the line of travel he was convinced the kidnappers took. Four horses there were, all of them shod. Actual tracks were few and far between, but Cap found enough—and those individual enough that he was sure he would recognize them again if ever he found fresh, clear imprints—that he did not doubt they were following the men who'd taken Rebecca.

Now. . . .

"Damn," he mumbled again, a little louder now that he was beyond George's hearing.

He knew what he could expect to find. The signs were clear enough. Two vultures high overhead. Or maybe three, he wasn't sure about that. One dark speck high in the atmosphere might have been a third carrion eater or might as easily have been a mote floating on the surface of Cap's own eye. Two, three, that did not matter. The birds were there. And down closer to the ground he could see magpies gathered like so many bundles of gaudy black and white on the upper branches of some scrub oak growing on the hillside Cap was approaching now.

Vultures, magpies, there was something dead over there. Something the birds could not reach else they would be on the ground feeding.

Covered over, he suspected, but the birds knew anyway. The birds always knew. No one knew for sure just how and why the birds knew such things. Not really. Some thought they could smell the stink of decay from afar. Cap did not think so. His own theory, right or wrong, was that the birds could see the clouds of flies that gathered over anything that was dead, whether lying in the open or lightly covered. It took a deep burial to keep the flies away. Cap suspected the vultures and the magpies looked for the faint gleam of sunlight catching the wings of the flies—he'd noticed as much himself when the sun was just right a time or two—and gathered to it in the sure certainty of finding a meal.

And now, here, the birds waited patiently for something else, a coyote or fox or badger, whatever, to expose the dead thing so they could reach it.

Dead thing. But not some mere thing. Not a dead mule deer or antelope or some other creature of the wild. Rebecca, Cap concluded, his heart heavy and sorrow already filling his chest near to overflowing. Dear Rebecca. Sweet and innocent and trusting. Gone west to see the buffalo and the wild Indians and the wonders her beloved grandpa told her stories about. Dead now. It would be Rebecca, he was sure. Had been sure since before they began this sad and hopeless search.

Cap rode slowly ahead, in no hurry to confirm what he expected, what he feared.

Damn them.

His hand, gnarled and liver-spotted, involuntarily tightened on the stock of the shiny new Winchester that lay unscabbarded in his lap, just as long ago he'd carried a muzzle-loading plains rifle from the St. Louis gun works of the Hobbs brothers.

"Damn those men," Cap whispered softly into the heat of the afternoon. And this time it was not a curse but a prayer. "Damn them, Lord. Please."

Chapter Thirteen

Cap rode up to the fire his son-in-law had built for their noon meal. The old man's expression was set, hard as stone and no more revealing. It did not have to be, though, to tell the tale. The travois that now dragged behind his horse told that story clearly enough. That and the bundle carried on the travois, wrapped in Cap's own blanket and tied tightly closed.

"Oh my God, I—"

"Don't, George. Don't," Cap said as the distraught father rushed to his elder child's body.

"Is it . . . ?"

"Yes, of course."

Brenn began clutching at the knots that held the rough woolen shroud closed over his child's lifeless features.

Cap scrambled hurriedly down from his saddle and intruded between George and the still form on the travois. "Don't, George. I'm giving you good advice here. Don't look. Don't try and see what they

59

done to her. It won't help you nor her nor Margaret. There's little enough dignity left to our little girl. Let her keep what of it she can."

"But I can't . . . just . . ."

"We'll bury her, George. You and me. We'll bury her here and go on. Believe me, that's for the best."

Brenn gave the old man an uncomprehending look that stretched on for several long moments as he tried to assimilate all that Cap was telling him. After a bit he shuddered, as if awakening with his mind still clogged and groggy from a nightmare. He blinked. "I can't . . . I have to take her back, Poppa Marsden. We have to bury her. In a proper cemetery and with a Christian service. Her mother will insist on it. We have to turn back now. We have to take . . ." his voice thickened and for a moment he had to struggle to continue. "We have to take my baby home."

Cap nodded. "You do what you have to, George. Take her back to Margaret. I'll ride on."

"But—"

"You won't get lost, George. From here you couldn't hardly get lost no matter what. Just ride straight south. By and by you'll find the railroad. Wait there. Flag down a train. They'll see you home."

"But what about you? What should I tell Margaret about where you'll be?"

"Tell her whatever you like. The truth, I suppose. The men that did this to Rebecca are out ahead somewhere. I'll be behind them. Soon or late, George, I'll be with them."

"We have an idea what they look like, Poppa Marsden. We can wire to law officers all through the territory. Someone will find them."

"Send out your wires when you get back to the telegraph, George. It can't hurt."

"But you won't go back with me, Poppa Marsden?"

"No, George. I can't do Rebecca any good by seeing her buried. I'll visit her grave later. When I can tell her that the men haven't gone unpunished for their sins."

"I don't know, Poppa Marsden. I don't like this."

"Neither of us does, son. But we'll both do what has to be done." Cap motioned toward the horse he'd been riding, the one with the travois tied onto it. "You can take this mount, George. Easier than switching the drag from one horse to the other. Take the supplies too. I won't need them. Not so long as I have a rifle and a knife."

"Your blanket . . ."

"I've done with a lot less than this before, George. I'll be fine. You tell Margaret that, will you? And tell her . . . I'll see her directly. We can go then and put flowers on Rebecca's resting place. Something bright and pretty and gay. You tell her that for me, George."

"I will, Poppa Marsden. I will."

"Fine. Thank you, George." Cap took his bedroll, thinner than it had been, from behind the cantle of the horse, and moved it to the saddle of the animal George had been riding. He transferred their entire bundle of foodstuffs onto the travois beside Rebecca's body and made sure everything was secured in place, then stepped into the saddle of the unencumbered mount.

"Aren't you even going to wait to have something to eat, Poppa Marsden?"

"Time enough for that later, George." Cap leaned down from the saddle and offered his son-in-law his hand. "Good-bye, George. And mind now. Ride south until you find the rails. I doubt you could miss them."

Frank Roderus

George nodded, mute, his expression strained. He said nothing as the old man rode away, leaving George alone in the wilderness with the body of his firstborn.

Chapter Fourteen

It was a vile and ugly thing that brought him here. But, God help him, Cap felt his heart lift with a sense of exhilaration, of long-unreleased freedom, as he rode farther away from George and the rails and the last vestiges of civilization.

It had been . . . how many years since he'd taken a horse and ridden alone into a wilderness? Half a lifetime ago. More. Now the old feelings came back to him as hour by hour he left the sere and arid sage scrub behind and below and climbed ever so slowly onto the high rolling grasslands that stretched from one horizon to the next.

Behind him lay the Wind River range, north were the majestic Big Horns, and ahead of him was a vast emptiness that, no matter how large, would prove too small to hide the men who'd murdered Cap's grandchild.

And in the meantime . . . in the meantime, God, he felt free and young and full of himself again as if he were still the boy—oh, he'd fancied himself a

63

man at the time, hadn't he—the boy who used to ride this same great and empty country.

Cap. The name itself was a source of pride to him, although that was not a thing he would have admitted aloud, not to anyone. For Cap was no mere nickname. It was a title proudly won and justly carried. Cap. It stood for captain, and so he once had been. Captain of a fur brigade. At twenty-three the youngest leader of free trappers in the mountains, elected from among them, selected by his fellows, voted to the fore by reason of skill and daring and determination.

In truth he had not been the most skilled trapper among them, nor the best tracker, not even the finest trader. But no man could match Cap's abilities with a rifle or a tomahawk and, more to the point, no one could match the steel of Old Marsden's will.

Old Marsden. Then the name had been a joke. Old at twenty-three, ha ha.

Now—he scarcely could believe it—old was what he was, and Cap was what he was called.

Old Cap. He frowned at the thought. Old he was, and he realized it whenever he looked into a mirror. But funny how seldom he felt old. Oh, to be sure, there were the achings in his joints whenever he woke and swung his scrawny legs off the side of a soft and cushy bed. That, he supposed, was a sign of being old.

But he didn't *feel* old. Not inside his head, he didn't. He still looked out on the world through the same eyes he'd had when he was fifteen, sixteen years old. And somewhere there inside himself he continued to believe he was still the same quick and vigorous soul he'd been those long years gone.

Old Cap. No one called him that anymore. Not since he'd become Old Cap in fact as well as in name. Funny thing, that. Old Cap had been an honor when he was in his twenties. Old Cap now would have been a reminder.

Still, he was not so old that his determination was gone. Nor so old that he would shrink away from tasks once set. Not so old that he would fail to find those men and settle with them for what they'd done to Rebecca.

That was a thing they would learn. Whoever they were.

Chapter Fifteen

It was five days after finding Rebecca's thin and battered body before Cap again found signs of people other than the ones he wanted. With the Big Horns looming rugged and handsome to the west, he came to the twin ruts of the military road that nowadays was called the Bozeman Trail, although it had been a common route of passage long before anyone had bothered to name it. Cap turned north on the Bozeman and remembered well before he reached it the flow of a nameless sweet water creek that came tumbling down from the mountains and joined, somewhere far to the east and south, the flow of the North Platte.

Tongue-tied Johnny Faraday started a trading post on the south bank of the creek once, Cap recalled. Johnny stuttered so bad he couldn't hardly talk with a white man, but he was hell for fluent when it came to the sign language of the plains tribes. Perhaps because of that, Johnny always seemed more comfortable among Indians than other whites. Cap hadn't thought of Tongue-tied Johnny in years. He wondered now what ever became of him. Or, for that matter, of the rest of the old crowd that used to populate this seemingly empty land.

It seemed almighty hard to believe, but now that he thought of it, Cap realized that all those boys would now be old men too. Those who'd survived, anyway. For all Cap knew, he might well be among the last of them around. Not quite the very last, of course. He knew Bridger was still alive. He smiled when he thought about Bridger. Old Gabe. Son of a buck was a fine hand when it came to telling lies, he was. Always had been. Nowadays Cap read some of Gabe's tall windies in the eastern newspapers that found their way to Santa Fe. Seemed Gabe had himself a trading post somewhere out in the South Pass country and made a living there by trading a little and talking a lot.

Some of those tales in the newspapers Cap recognized, although not all of them had Bridger in the middle of them to begin with, never mind how they sounded now that Bridger was the one doing the telling.

The truth, though, was that Cap didn't mind the "improvements" Gabe might've made from the original versions, not even the ones that inserted Bridger into a few tight spots that Cap himself lived through half a lifetime back.

It was all fair game, he reckoned, and no harm done if some eastern writer fellow came to Bridger's scent stick and stepped into the set Gabe laid for him. No harm at all, the way Cap saw it.

He was deep in such thought when he topped a rise in the road and saw with considerable wonderment that Tongue-tied Johnny's old cabin was still there.

It sat out in the open now, although Cap remembered it as being built amid a grove of tall cottonwoods, and the post had been added onto over the years.

Johnny built only a long, double-length cabin with most of the inside devoted to trading and a small part at the west end divided off for living purposes. The cabin was built facing south to take advantage of what sun-warmth was available during the winters, with protection from the wind being supplied by the nearby trees.

Those cottonwoods were gone now, and the ground around the old cabin was bare and beaten, most of it contained inside corral fencing and a wagon park for the benefit of passing freighters.

Wind protection, what little of it there was, seemed to be provided by stacks of firewood cut and split and piled on the west and north sides of the cabin. There wasn't much left of the cordwood at this time of year, and someone would have some serious work ahead to lay in enough wood supply for the coming winter, but it was easy to see where last year's wood had been and where this year's would go.

Several sheds had been added close to the creek, but it was amazing how clearly Cap recalled now the way it all had been when Johnny built it, how familiar the old place still was to him.

He wondered . . . naw, surely it wasn't possible that old Tongue-tied Johnny was still alive and still running the place.

Of course that would not be possible. Cap knew that.

But he couldn't help feeling a small thrill of excitement as he bumped his horse into a lope for the last quarter mile to the old trading post.

Chapter Sixteen

"Who'd you say, old man?"

Cap repeated Johnny's name for him.

The trader shook his head. "Never heard of him."

"It isn't important," Cap said, hiding the unexpected disappointment he felt. "He was . . . never mind."

"You want something, mister? A drink? Little bacon? Anything?"

"I could use a few things," Cap said, deciding to sweeten the conversation with a little commercial activity. The trader who'd taken Tongue-tied Johnny's place did not seem overfriendly, and Cap doubted the dark-eyed, greasy-haired so-and-so would volunteer much if answers were the only items a passing stranger was interested in carrying away when he pulled out.

Cap made up an order off the top of his head, food items for the most part, and tea. Funny how he found himself wanting tea again after years of drinking nothing but coffee—well, for a hot beverage anyway—down home in Santa Fe. Back in the old days it had been easier to buy, or to make, tea than coffee, due largely to the darn Englishers with all their activity in the north country. Once he left the mountains, Cap nearly forgot the scent and the flavor of tea brewing on a cold morning. Now it came back to him and he found himself wanting a taste of the brisk, bitter drink again.

"That's all?" the trader asked.

"Ayuh, I expect it will do."

The trader turned away to begin picking items off his shelves. Cap spoke to the man's back, his voice offhand and casual. "By the by, friend, you wouldn't happen to've seen three men and a pack-horse pass through here, would you?"

"Why d'you ask?"

"Nothing much, really. For the past couple days I been running into their sign. I thought if we were all traveling in the same direction, I'd like to see if I could hook up with them. For protection, like."

The trader turned and eyed him. "Good idea. An old man like you, out here all alone, you could get yourself hurt, all right."

Cap seethed but knew better than to let it show. Get himself hurt. Huh! Why, he'd traipsed this whole stretch of country, knew it like the palm of his own hand. And before this ignorant pup was ever birthed. Get himself hurt, indeed.

"The party you asked about did stop in here," the trader said. "Headed south on the road from here, if that helps you any, mister."

"South? That doesn't make sense. Why'd they come so far north just to turn south again?"

"Now, mister, that's something I expect you'd have to ask them. It wasn't my business, and I didn't question them about it. Maybe they wandered too far north. Maybe they have to meet somebody on the road and wanted to be sure and not miss the other party. I dunno the answer. All I can tell you is what they said to me when they was here."

Cap grunted and shrugged. He couldn't see that the post trader had any reason to lie about it. It looked to him like he would have to turn back south toward Cheyenne now if he wanted to find Rebecca's murderers.

He thanked the trader, paid for his supplies, and went back out to the horse George had hired for him.

Chapter Seventeen

Cap squatted close to a fire hardly bigger than would have fit—a trifle uncomfortably—onto the palm of his hand. A trio of flat stones served as a tripod to support the tin can he was using as a tea mug. The water came to a rolling boil and Cap dropped a generous pinch of tea leaves into the cup, then quickly pulled the fire apart and scattered the embers. Not that there was any particular need for stealth here, but the habit of caution was strong.

Funny, he thought, how quickly those old habits were returning now. He hadn't had need to hide his smoke for . . . what? . . . thirty years or so? Didn't really need to now either, of course. But the simple truth was that he would have felt almighty nervous to be hunkered down on this hillside calling attention to himself.

Down below and a good half mile distant, he could plainly see the wagons parked in the trading post yard. He felt reasonably sure the freighters intended to move on before dark, since they hadn't broken their hitches or moved the livestock into the corrals.

And since those boys seemed likely to move on, well, he would just wait here where he was and opt for a mite of privacy.

He had no need to speak with the bullwhackers. He'd done that already yesterday evening. He recognized the rigs easy enough, and there was nothing more they might say that he needed to hear.

More to the point, it might well be for the best if there weren't any witnesses handy when he had his next little talk with the man who'd taken over Tongue-tied Johnny's old store and buildings.

Better, Cap thought, to stay out here where he was. Maybe spend some time remembering Rebecca. How sweet she'd been. How young. And how innocent.

Cap poured a dollop of molasses into his tea, just like in the old days, when dry sugar was hard to find and harder to transport without it going damp and lumpy. He stirred the mixture idly with a twig while his thoughts ranged back in time by a few weeks.

He could as good as see little Rebecca at the dinner table back in Omaha, so childlike and dear. So interested in her grandpap's yarns and so full of a thirst to know and to see all the things he'd talked about.

It was, Cap felt in some small, deep corner of himself, his fault that Rebecca had ridden the train west with her daddy.

It was his fault the child had suffered and died.

His fault. And that of the men who sooner or later would have to answer for the things they'd done to that little girl.

And no one, no one at all, was going to stand in the way of the retribution those men earned when they violated that child.

No one.

Chapter Eighteen

It was coming dark when Cap once again dismounted outside the old trading post and tied his horse to a corral rail close by the door. Lights had been showing inside the store for near on a half hour now, and he could no longer see any dust raised by the northbound freight wagons that had pulled out several hours past.

Once inside the store, Cap propped his rifle beside the door and removed his hat, holding it diffidently at his belly as he approached the man behind the counter.

The trader—Cap never had got his name—was not alone, however. There was a girl with him. An Indian girl, young and thin and filthy. Cap had no idea what tribe the girl might be from. She wore a faded gingham dress and a ratty scrap of shawl that might have been white a generation or so back. She was barefoot. The dress was cut so that it barely came to knee-length on her. There was little enough doubt about her function here. Part of the merchandise. When Cap came in, she and the proprietor were standing belly to belly, and Cap got the impression he'd interrupted the good merchant's intent to sample his own wares.

"Back again, I see," the trader said, this time with no hint of welcome in his voice.

"Ayuh."

"You want to buy something, that's fine. I can't tell you more than I already done. If you want information, get outta here."

"Reckon I'll buy," Cap told him.

The trader sighed. Loudly, pointedly, making no effort to hide his impatience. "All right then, if you got to."

Cap smiled and nodded. He smiled at the girl too, and sketched a few motions in the air.

"What was that?" the trader demanded.

Cap's expression did not change. "I just told her hello. Hope you don't mind." In fact what he'd said was, *Leave in peace, child. Now.*

"Don't do that no more," the trader demanded.

"All right."

The girl said something too soft for Cap to hear, then turned and slipped outside as if in a sudden hurry to visit the backhouse.

Once they were alone in the trading post, Cap ambled closer to the store counter.

"What do you need?" the trader wanted to know.

"I'm buying information," Cap told him.

"The hell you are. I told you that already."

"All right," Cap agreed. "I'm willing to buy. If you don't want to sell then I expect I'll just have to take what I need anyway."

Too late, the man began to give his visitor an increasingly nervous reassessment.

Too late because by then Cap was close to him. Close enough to reach out and, seemingly without haste, take a firm grip on the trader's shirtfront. Close enough that the trader did not so much as see the knife slide out of Cap's belt. Close enough, however, that he felt the implied bite of the blade as it came to rest pressing lightly against his trembling Adam's apple.

The man made a very slight gurgling sound.

"In case you're wondering, neighbor, there's not hardly any end to what I'll do to get the information I want. Do you understand me, friend? Real, *real* plain now?"

"I, uh . . . um, I . . ." Sweat beaded the man's forehead, and his complexion became as pale as candle wax.

The knife blade pressed fractionally harder on his flesh.

"Wh—whatever you say. Sir."

Cap nodded and, his voice calm and mild, sounding in no way angered or upset, he commenced asking questions.

Chapter Nineteen

The fellow should have left well enough alone. He really should have.

They were done. Finished. Cap was walking away, entirely willing to turn his back on this whole ugly episode and forget about this man who called himself Manning Jewison.

According to Jewison, the three men who'd passed through several days back, the ones who so obviously had to be the men who'd violated and murdered Cap's grandbaby, were Everett Shear, Tom Rayne, and another man known to Jewison only as Coffee.

Shear and Rayne were old compadres of the trader, Jewison claimed, and he hadn't wanted to peach on them.

They had admitted—albeit without any details being confided—the possibility that someone might be on their trail. Jewison claimed he did not know why Cap wanted them. Nor did he want to know.

Cap told him anyway, not that the revelation seemed to bring about any discernible change of heart in Manning Jewison. The man's willingness to talk seemed to be in direct proportion to the pressure of Cap's knife edge against his throat. That and by the thought of what future steps might be undertaken by this elderly—but far from frail—visitor.

"I'm being straight with you, mister. I swear it t'you, I swear."

"I hope for your sake, friend, that you're telling me the truth. Otherwise I'll come back here for a third visit. Somehow I don't think you'd want me to do that."

"No, I . . . ." Jewison swallowed, the slight motion enough to leave a crease indented into his flesh where the steel blade lay. Cap watched with mild interest as the crease darkened and then began to disappear as the flow of blood filled out the flesh beneath the elastic surface of the man's skin. Skin, Cap noticed, that was overdue for an application of soap and water.

"You were saying?" Cap prompted.

"I . . . already told you. Everything I know. Everything. I swear it, mister."

"Uh-huh."

"North. They're headed for the Milk River country. Gonna do some trading up there, they said. With the Indians. They asked me . . . you know. Prices. What goods move the best. Like that. Said they were gonna buy a load of stuff, trade goods, like that, at Bailey's Landing on the Missoura. You know it?"

Cap shook his head.

"Below the Milk. You can't miss it. There's . . . a ferry. Take you across. That's where they said they were going. But they asked me—we're old friends, them and me—they asked me to not let on to anybody. That's why I told you they turned south. I . . . didn't mean you harm. Nor the kid neither. I didn't have anything to do with that."

Cap nodded. "I know. That's the reason you're still alive, friend." He smiled and the knife slid back behind his belt. "No hard feelings, right?"

"Right, damn right," Jewison agreed.

Cap stood looking at him for a moment, then said, "I trust we won't meet again."

"No, I . . . there's no reason for that. I told you true. I swear it."

Cap grunted and turned away, his posture loose and the heavy Winchester trailing butt-down in his left hand. It was plain enough that no matter what, the rifle was no immediate threat.

Cap wondered even as he strode lightly toward the door and the new-fallen night beyond it just how much grit this puffing, sweating Jewison had.

He found out when he was yet three paces from the door.

He heard the distinctive, faintly oily *cla-clack* of a hammer being cocked.

Jewison was frightened enough, or to give the man some due, perhaps was loyal enough to his chums, that he was intent on making a try.

He really should have left well enough alone.

Cap whirled at the first sound.

Jewison, still behind his store counter, had a Springfield rifle in his hands. Not one of the outmoded muzzle-loaders, but a converted musket with the newly designed trapdoor breech to accept metallic cartridges.

The half-inch bore of the big gun loomed large as a cannon's mouth, and the impact from one of those thumb-sized slugs could pick a man up and set him down elsewhere.

If he stood still and let himself be shot.

Cap's expression changed. Not to rage. He'd more than half expected this result, darn it. But to something akin to sorrow. This was not a thing he'd wanted to do, never mind that Jewison tried to shield Rebecca's murderers from retribution. As he'd pointed out himself, Jewison hadn't been involved in that.

Still, the man had chosen to take a hand in the game now, and there was nothing Cap could do to dissuade him.

He'd already had his chances. And used them up.

Jewison gave Cap a biting look of smug triumph as he raised the Springfield and swung the barrel on line with the old man's belly.

Perhaps he had time to see and to wonder that Cap did not even try to raise his own rifle.

But then perhaps he did not, for Jewison had time enough for only a few scant heartbeats.

The tomahawk worn by the old mountain man sped through the air, revolving in a lazy midair spin that presented the sharpened blade flush on Jewison's breastbone.

The weight of the iron ax head sliced through cartilage, twisted to the side a mite as it glanced off bone, and buried itself deep in Jewison's chest.

The trader looked down, growing horror in his suddenly wide eyes as he saw the wooden ax haft protruding from his flesh.

He probably had time enough to know that he was killed.

Then his eyes glazed and the life seeped out of him in a rush. He collapsed onto the swept-earth floor of old Tongue-tied Johnny's trading post, blood pouring out of his body to mingle with the dirt where he lay. The Springfield fell with a clatter, the impact of its fall dropping the hammer to fill the store with the roar of a gunshot and the peculiarly acrid stink of gunpowder burnt inside an enclosed space. The errant ball did no harm so far as Cap could see. Not that he cared enough to investigate beyond what was obvious.

With a sigh, he went back the way he had just come, stepped around behind the counter and—he had to tug twice and give the handle a twist to force the dead man's flesh to give up its hold on the tomahawk—retrieved the rather innocent-looking hand ax.

There were not, Cap reflected, a whole lot of folks left these days who properly appreciated the value of a plain old trading pattern tomahawk.

He used a bolt of Jewison's red calico trade cloth to clean the blood off the blade, and dropped the ax back into his belt.

Over by the door he could see the Indian girl peering warily into the store.

Go home, Cap signed to her. *Take whatever you want from here and leave in peace.*

Do you need a place to hide? she returned in the universal sign language.

Wolf Who Sings Loud does not hide, Cap responded, the half-forgotten name returning now in a hand-phrase long familiar. *If any look for me, child, tell the truth. No harm should come to you.*

I would hide you if you wish.

Cap thanked her and shook his head. *There are things I must do now.*

He gathered that Manning Jewison hadn't been one of this girl's favorite people. No surprise, that.

Cap told the girl good-bye and once again turned toward the door.

The night air smelled good to him when he reached it. Clean and fresh after the stink of blood and gunpowder.

He retrieved his horse and set out onto the military road regardless of the hour. It was not that he felt any sense of urgency now. Just that he wanted shut of old Johnny's trading post and hoped he need never stop there again. Killing was not new to him. But it was something in which he could take no pleasure.

Three times more. Three more deaths.

And then, he hoped, never again.

Chapter Twenty

The Milk was an awful long way from the gold discoveries that the man said they were headed for when they were back down at Benson Creek.

But then men had been known to lie before. And who were they more likely to tell the truth to, some casually met strangers in a railhead saloon, or an old friend with whom they were passing time and asking for protection, just in case John Law might come a-calling?

The ruts of the well-defined freight road swung west somewhere above the bluecoat fort—Cap hadn't stopped there and did not know what the place was called—built just below the ridge where once long ago Cap dropped a mighty fine-tasting bull elk calf. He remembered that elk in particular because he'd later swapped its hide to the Crow named Two Fingers in exchange for Two Fingers's eldest daughter, Bessie Beaucoup.

That hadn't been her proper name. Cap could no longer remember what that was. Bessie Beaucoup was what he'd called her.

Cap had to smile a little, thinking about that darn Bessie. He'd gotten her cheap. And she'd been way overpriced at that. The woman had a tongue on her sharp enough to slice meat, and a temper as volatile as any French grind priming powder.

He didn't make it halfway through the winter with her before he kicked her out. Tried to swap her to someone, anyone, for something, anything, but all the other boys in the brigade knew her tantrums and not even Cecil Knott—who once claimed, with a good weight of argument on his side, to be the ugliest man in the Shining Mountains—wanted to take Bessie Beaucoup into his lodge. Cap ended up sending her back to her family and counted the deal a dead loss.

Still, that little elk had sure been tender and sweet to the taste.

All of that was long ago now, he reflected, as he rode by without pause. He expected most of the boys he'd trapped with that season were dead and gone now.

He thought about them and about the times when he'd been young and the country empty save for a few Indians and even fewer white men. It had been good then, but that was past, and things were different now.

Better now, he supposed, but if he was pressed on the point, he would have had to admit that he was just as happy he wouldn't have to see what the discovery of gold had done to a country that had been paradise when he'd known it. Somewhere out past the Madison, they said. Fine country that had been.

No, he wasn't at all anxious to see how "civilization" had gone and improved on it.

The wagon road turned west and Cap continued

north toward where the Milk River came down to join the Missouri.

There was supposed to be a fort there too, he'd heard. Peck? He thought maybe that was it.

And a landing called Bailey's, according to the recently deceased Mr. Jewison.

Lordy, but he hoped the trader had been telling him the truth about that.

Everett Shear. Tom Rayne. Coffee. The names burned deep in Cap's memory, and the thought of them made his gut clench tight in anticipation.

Everett Shear. Tom Rayne. Coffee.

He would find them. Not the least flicker of doubt ever entered his mind on that score. Wherever they went, however long it took, he would find them.

Everett Shear. Tom Rayne. Coffee.

Chapter Twenty-one

"Mmm, don't rush me now," the bearded fat man said, fingernails probing deep inside the reddish-blond fur that matted his face. The storekeeper thought for several long moments, then shook his head. "No, sir, I can't say I know of a place hereabouts called Bailey's Landing. And I been here as long as any. Longer than most. No, can't say that I do. Though now that I think on it . . . let me see . . . there was a man named Bailey. Laid claim to some land a couple miles upstream along the Milk. A woodlot, it was. He cut timber and floated it down to the Missoura to split and sell to the riverboat trade. I dunno as I ever heard his place called Bailey's Landing, but I suppose a body could call it that if they was of a mind to."

"That could be the place the fellow meant," Cap conceded. He had already determined that the three men he wanted had not been seen around Fort Peck. Or anyway had not done anything to make themselves memorable. Nor did anyone here seem to know the men by name. Bailey's Landing seemed his next best bet. Either that or start riding up the Milk and hope for the best.

The fat man shrugged. "Could be what you want, sure. Bailey. What was that man's name anyhow? George? Maybe. He's been dead, oh, four years now? Maybe longer. I didn't know him well, you understand, though you can't live around here and not at least know of everybody else whether you're friends with them or not. This Bailey, he wasn't a prayerful sort, if you see what I mean. Drank hard spirits, smoked tobacco, like that. Me, I took the temperance oath when I was still a boy. Never backslid on it either. I don't care to associate with men like Bailey was. You're temperance yourself, are you?" the man asked with a broad, knowing smile, as if trying to identify a brother lodge member or such.

Cap frowned a little. He couldn't help himself. He disapproved of crude language on general principles and if pressed would have acknowledged that he expected there was a God. Somewhere. But Cap also enjoyed the flavor of a good whiskey on his tongue and the warmth of it in his belly. And he thought it only fair to give other men the freedom of their own preferences just as he firmly believed others darn well better give him the freedom of his. He certainly did not want to get into a debate on the evils of liquor with some backwoods teetotaler who had nits in his beard and like as not nits in his thinking as well.

"Upriver a few miles you said?" Cap prompted, trying to direct the fellow's train of thought back onto helpful lines.

"Somewhere up there. I couldn't say exactly how far."

"But this Bailey is dead now?"

"So they say. Somebody found him in his cabin one spring a couple years back. Been dead long enough to dry out, I heard. Don't know what he come to die of, but a man alone . . ." The fat man shrugged again. "You know how it is."

"Sure," Cap agreed. And indeed he did. A man alone could go under in country like this, even as built-up and civilized as it was becoming nowadays, and no one would ever be the wiser. More than a few of Cap's old friends rode away from rendezvous in the old days and were never heard of again. They might have died by accident or of illness, been killed by Indians . . . or simply wandered off to California and took a notion to stay there. A man never knew. "Sure," Cap repeated. "I know how that is all right."

"If there's anything I can do for you? Anything you need?" The fat man motioned toward the shelving behind him where his wares were displayed.

Mostly to twist the fellow's tail a mite, Cap said, "I'll take a small keg of trade whiskey if you have one. Or plain alcohol. I expect I'd still know how to brew up some popskull."

The fat man surprised him. "I have either one. Which d'you prefer?"

Cap kept his expression bland, but his eyes might have twinkled just a little. The stuff was too vile to partake of, he thought, but apparently there was nothing in this man's book of rules that said he couldn't take a little profit by trafficking in whiskey.

"How much for a couple gallons of the ready-made?"

It wasn't that he was developing all that powerful a thirst exactly. But a gallon or two of whiskey might well help him find Shear and Rayne and the man who called himself Coffee. Cap was getting into country now where he thought that just might be a help, and he was willing to invest a few dollars in the possibility, just in case.

Chapter Twenty-two

He found the place where Bailey had lived. At least he assumed that was it, judging from what the helpful fellow downriver had said. There had been a cabin, couple of outbuildings, the remains of a very old dugout that might have been here before Bailey came along. Now there wasn't much left of any of them. Cottonwood rots away quickly anyhow, even when it is in active use and under constant repair, and once the roof fell in, the rest of the cabin had gone downhill at a rapid pace. Cap had seen the like before. It made a man feel worn out and old before his time, somehow, seeing the structures of man melt into the ground practically as soon as the men who made them turned their backs. Or, in this case, returned to the ground before them.

If Bailey was buried here, Cap could find no sign of that, so perhaps he'd been taken elsewhere for burial. After all, there once was a time when whites hid their graves from red Indians, but there was no need for that sort of thing anymore. Not to preserve the dead from being despoiled by enemies nor to hide the fact that there was one less rifle available come the next skirmish between two implacable foes in different-colored skins.

Cap looked carefully around the place that had been Bailey's Landing, but if his fugitives stopped here they did it briefly and without leaving any sign that Cap could identify.

He stopped long enough to strip some dry-rotted wood out of the remains of a shed and use it to build a fire—smokeless from habit rather than necessity—and made himself some tea and lunch while he pondered.

The three men who'd murdered Rebecca still could be somewhere up the Milk. Just because Bailey was dead, well, they might not have known of that. And if they needed to provision themselves with food or trading materials, those could be gotten almost anywhere along the Missouri these days. It wasn't like back in the old times when a man could go weeks or even months without sight of another white. Now you would have to make a determined effort to get more than a few days travel from the nearest post or farm or trading point.

Things just weren't the way they used to be.

Which, Cap conceded, was mostly for the good.

But now . . . now he needed to find those three. And now there were altogether too many dang possible places where they could have gone.

He considered what course to take from here while he packed up and scattered his fire so it would have taken a man well-versed in woodlore to ever know someone was recently around.

Cap was two days upriver from Bailey's Landing the next time he saw a human being.

And then it was only by woeful mischance.

His horse stepped out of a crackwillow thicket and walked practically into a bevy of naked, splashing little Indian boys who were bathing in a sand-bottomed pool in a bend of the river.

That part was all right.

What gave Cap a spurt of heartburn was the fact that those kids' mommas and daddies were close by also. And the daddies looked to all be armed with thoroughly modern rifles.

Oh for the good old days, Cap thought, when you could mostly count on facing Indians who had nothing better than bows to shoot with. Short-range bows.

He blanched pale, cussing himself for being so lost in thought as to walk into a situation like this, and wondered if his best bet was to turn his horse and run like mad.

Or grin and try to talk his way through.

He glanced around behind and saw that running wasn't apt to accomplish much.

Coming up in the rear was a party of five—no, six, he could see another one skulking along in the thick brush now—six young warriors with mud streaking their faces much like the gaudy warpaint of old and with short-barreled muskets in their hands.

Cap was caught between the two parties, the young bucks behind, and the mature warriors in front.

He felt an electric tingle begin to prickle at the nape of his neck as if he were getting a series of light shocks of the sort you get in winter when you walk on a wool rug, except they were coming one on the heels of another.

He could feel the hair lift at the back of his neck, and it was all he could do to stay loose and easy in the saddle when what he really wanted to do was wheel around and larrup right away from there.

From somewhere came a fleeting memory of the story he'd told to Rebecca and little Cathy at dinner back in Omaha. How he'd been trapped fair and square by the Blackfeet.

Well, they had him again, it looked like.

And this time there was no box canyon to climb his way out of. This time there was nothing stouter than a willow switch to hide behind.

What had that darn George said at the time? Oh, yes. He'd laughed and claimed Cap was going to tell the children that old yarn about how the Indians killed him.

He rather hoped George Brenn hadn't been prescient when he came up with that one.

Cap swallowed, then nudged his horse into a slow walk directly toward the men who were standing, guns ready, on the east bank of the Milk River.

Chapter Twenty-three

The headman, or so Cap judged him to be, was a wrinkled and gnarled old goat, so sun-dried and shrunken he looked like he could have fit into Cap's coat pocket . . . with room enough left over to put an apple in there with him. He was bent over with age and infirmity and he had to lean on a decorated staff to remain upright, or as close to that as he seemed capable of getting, but his eyes were clear and penetrating.

Cap reined the horse to a stop in front of the old man and raised his left hand in a cautious greeting. The other hand remained loose but darn well ready lying on the grip of the Winchester rifle in his lap.

I am Wolf Who Sings Loud, Cap signed to him. *I know your people from long ago. Who are you?*

You are Coyote Howling, the old Indian returned. Then he laughed. *I have heard you sing. You are Coyote Howling.*

Do I know you, Grandfather?

You do not remember me, Coyote Howling? I am

Climbs High. Two times I have fired my arrows at you, Coyote Howling. Two times I missed my aim. I see your medicine is still strong. You are alive. My warriors and I, we killed most of your kind. Do you not remember me?

Cap felt something twist in his belly. A sense of sadness, mostly. This feeble, gray-haired old man was Climbs High? Cap remembered Climbs High as a warrior, deadly and cunning. One of the fiercest and most proud of the Blackfoot tribe.

This was the exact same band—or what was left of them; Cap saw very few of them standing now on the bank of the Milk River—that trapped him in that box canyon close by the Musselshell those many years ago.

The same band that killed poor Billy Hargrew. And like to got Cap too. He'd been lucky that time.

But . . . this ancient, doddering old blanket Indian was the proud and ferocious Climbs High?

Cap hoped his expression did not reveal the pity that he felt.

He'd heard, of course, that the Blackfeet were laid low. A disease, he'd heard. The pox or some version of it. They said the Blackfeet were near wiped out by an epidemic of whatever it was. Said there were whole bands that laid down and died with no one left to bury the dead. Lodges were left standing with no one living even to burn them to kill the pestilence.

Cap had heard those things, but by then he was far away from this country, down in the warm Mexican south where there were no Blackfeet.

The last time he'd been north of what they now called Colorado Territory, the Blackfeet were still in their prime, still the most hostile and deadly of all the tribes. Bug's Boys, they'd been called then.

The Devil's Spawn. And other names much worse than those.

More than once Cap had fought these people. More than once Cap had fought old Climbs High. Now Climbs High looked so frail that a robust handshake might shatter the bones of his hand.

We were good enemies, Cap signed to Climbs High. That elicited a grin, exposing pale gums where teeth should have been.

Good enemies, Climbs High repeated. *Yes. Good enemies.* The old man laughed. *You will join us, Coyote Howling? Did you bring meat to share with us? Did you bring presents? Come. Join me in my lodge. I have a fat wife. She will feed you. Warm your blanket tonight if you like. Did you bring meat, yes?*

Cap grunted and stepped down off his horse. He had enough to share. Whatever he had these sad and hungry people were welcome to. He could always replace his things down at Fort Peck. Anywhere along the Missouri for that matter. Climbs High and his Blackfeet could not do that for themselves.

And in a way, what Cap said to the old man was true. They had been very good enemies indeed. Strong and worthy of the fear and respect they engendered back in the days of their youth. Now . . .

I would ask from you a favor, Climbs High, Cap signed, then opened his pack and laid everything out on the ground for the Blackfeet to share. *I am looking for three men. White men. I will describe them for you.*

Chapter Twenty-four

They weren't here. Climbs High and his Blackfeet swore it to be so, and they would surely have known. Bad off as they were, this band would be extra diligent when it came to seeking out strangers in their midst. If nothing else, the Blackfeet would welcome an opportunity to beg. Cap hated the thought of that. But he did not shy away from using the knowledge to his own advantage. He would certainly have used the Blackfeet to locate Rebecca's killers for him.

But they were not here. The only white men on the Milk this year had been a man in his thirties accompanied by his son of ten or so. The two had been searching for a strayed milk cow, which they failed to find, largely because it was already on drying racks at the Blackfoot camp.

Climbs High and his people, though, were sure there had been no others, no party anything like the three men Cap described, the three who were murderers.

The trader at Tongue-tied Johnny Faraday's post down south had lied. And now there was no going back to question him again. Cap scowled at the bad luck. If only the fool hadn't—but then Jewison knew at the time that he was lying, knew by lying he risked Cap's return and another, likely much more violent confrontation. No wonder the man tried to kill him back there, Cap realized now. In a manner of speaking, Jewison's attempt to shoot him in the back was pure self-defense, understandable enough now that he knew the others were not on the Milk after all.

So if not here, where?

Cap frowned. The gold camps? It was what they'd said back at the railhead. It may well have been the truth.

And the killers had no reason to think they were being pursued at this late date. By now the posse of railroad men would long since have turned back, gone back to their jobs and their whiskey and the rowdy comforts of end-of-track.

Poor George. Poor sad George. And Margaret. By now George would have his child's body back home in Omaha. By now Rebecca would have been buried with family and friends weeping over her grave.

Cap had no time for mourning. Not while the little girl's killers remained somewhere free and laughing, able to enjoy the sight of a sunrise or the scent on a mountain breeze.

Damn them, Cap silently intoned. His plea was not a curse but a request that he laid before whatever Almighty there was, whether that force be the stern God of the fire and brimstone preachers or the mystic Great Spirit of the Blackfeet and their kind.

Praying was not a thing Cap Marsden normally did. But now he once again begged the unknown and unknowable to damn those men who had murdered Rebecca. Begged that they be damned, yes, and that he be led to them so he could see retribution made. By his hand or by any other. It was not personal vengeance that Cap demanded, but simple justice. An eye for an eye or tooth for tooth . . . blood for blood, life for life.

Right now the ledger showed itself to be three deaths short of a balance, and Cap had no intention of turning back until the debt for little Rebecca's murder was paid off.

Thank you, Climbs High, Cap signed. *You make as good a friend as once you made an enemy*. The words seemed to please the old man.

Cap gave the Blackfeet all the food, tobacco, and tea he had with him, then turned south again, back toward the Missouri, where he could resupply and ask about the gold fields that lay somewhere, he had no idea where, to the west.

Chapter Twenty-five

Cap had no idea if George had bought the horse, rented it, borrowed it. It didn't matter. He sold the animal to the sutler at Fort Peck and with a clear conscience wrote out and signed a bill of sale. The horse would only have been an encumbrance to him now. Besides, he hadn't brought much in the way of cash with him when he'd hurriedly left Omaha. He could use the money from the horse to buy passage west on the next river steamer to come along, and afterward for transport on to Virginia City.

"Going to try your hand at prospecting, old-timer?" the sutler responded when Cap asked the man's advice about how best to reach the gold fields.

Cap only grunted in response.

"Gold is a young man's game," the bespectacled fellow told him. "Breaking rock, hauling buckets of stone, wading shin-deep in freezing water if you stake out a placer claim. It's hard work, mister. You might be better off to consider something else."

Cap doubted that placer mining, using a fluted pan and quicksilver amalgam to extract flake gold from the gravel of streambeds, was any wetter or colder than trapping for beaver in those selfsame streams had been. But then the sutler was right about one thing. Either of those should be considered a young man's pursuit. Cap took no offense at the comments in any event. The man was only trying to be helpful.

Nor did Cap feel obliged to explain the business that had brought him here. He listened patiently and went on with what needed doing. "You say there's no schedule for the boats heading upriver?"

"No way they can hold to a schedule. The river, she's a fickle bitch. Never know what to expect. Snags and deadheads and the channel changing from one trip to the next. No, there's no telling when a boat will come by. But you don't have to worry about missing anything. Listen for a steam whistle and head for the landing down there whenever you hear one. There's always room for one more aboard when a man has money in his hand."

Cap thanked the man and solicited one final piece of advice, where to find the best meal available locally. Then he picked up his few belongings and carried them out in search first of food, then of a place where he could sit and wait for a steamer bound west on these upper reaches of the great Missouri.

Chapter Twenty-six

"Will you *please* shut up?"

"I'm only trying to—"

"I know what you're trying to say. Now shut up, will you? Please?"

Cap scowled and grumbled, "For twenty dollars a man ought to be able—"

"Old man, I don't want to hear it no more. You been saying that same thing the whole way. Now drop it. Right now. Or get out and walk. One more word out of you, and I swear . . ."

Cap growled some more. But quietly.

It was unfair. Worse than unfair, it was robbery. Twenty dollars. Huh! To ride on a wagon. Not a proper coach even, but a clattering, creaking, rickety excuse for a dang freight wagon.

A dollar, fine. Even two or three. But twenty? It was pitiful the way men's heads turned to mush when they thought there was gold to be had. And even more pitiful the way people like this Simms fellow took advantage of the fools and robbed them.

It hurt Cap's pride to think he was being lumped in with the gold-crazed idjits who were willing to spend anything, everything in the faint hope they would find a pot of gold at the end of some fuzzy glimpse of rainbow.

And some rainbow this was. Cap judged Virginia City with a critical eye as the slow-moving wagon approached the town.

Town. So it was. Here in the middle of nothing there was suddenly a town. Cap was in awe of that fact. This was poor country by his reckoning. Never had any beaver to speak of, not in Cap's day it hadn't. Never was of any particular interest to Cap or his kind. And never would he have thought in this or half a dozen more lifetimes he would see the day that there was a town set here in these Dakota hills.

No, he reminded himself, this wasn't Dakota any more. It was Montana now. Fact remained, it was useless ground. Or would have been if someone hadn't gone and found gold here.

The question in Cap's mind wasn't so much if there was gold. It was wondering what sort of fool would have been wasting his time out here looking for the stuff.

Well, there was no accounting for taste, or so the man said when he kissed the cow.

"I wouldn't have paid twenty dollars to ride a comfortable railroad car here," Cap muttered half-under his breath.

"If there was a railroad built out here you wouldn't've had to. Now dry up, will you?"

Cap gave the freighter a withering look. Anyway one that would have been withering had the man been paying attention. "I don't suppose twenty dollars buys me your opinion about a place where a man can put up and find some decent food," he said.

"Old man, if you think I've treated you hard, just wait till you see what they charge for ordinary services in Virginia City these days." The driver turned his head away and spat. Cap knew he wasn't being courteous, though; it was just that he didn't want to spit into the wind. "A hotel room is five dollars a night. Meals start at a dollar and go up from there. You never been to a gold camp before now, mister?"

"Never wanted to. Wouldn't be in this one if I didn't have to."

"You're not here to get rich with all these other young rannies?"

"I'm already as rich as I expect to get. Which isn't very, mind you. No, I'm here on personal business."

"I see," the driver said, although he obviously didn't, not in the particulars at any rate.

Cap filled him in. The more people who knew why he was looking for the three men, he figured, the more cooperation he could expect. Cap might have no experience in gold camps, but he had more than a little experience when it came to men and their nature. And most men, no matter how hard, would not countenance anyone bringing harm to a child, anybody's child, nor to a woman who wasn't the batterer's own. A man could apply the rod to his own wife or child—or maybe to a whore if he didn't beat her too awfully bad—but not to any other. That simply was not done.

"I didn't know," Simms apologized when he'd heard. The next time he let fly a stream of tobacco juice it was well away from Cap's seat even though the breeze did not make him do it. Cap couldn't help but notice, however, that the abject sympathy did not prompt Simms to return any of the twenty-dollar fare Cap paid for his ride on the slow, miserable wagon.

"Tell you what," Simms said.

"Mmm?"

"I have a friend in town. He runs a saloon. Has some rooms in the back that he lets out sometimes. I'll ask him to help you out. Maybe give you a break on the room rent. You know? And better than that, you tell him what you just told me. Barney knows every saloonkeeper in Virginia City. He can pass the word around. If your men are here, Barney and his friends can find them for you if they're of a mind to."

"I'd appreciate that," Cap said, meaning it. If Simms meant what he said and this Barney fellow could help out, it would be worth a twenty-dollar wagon fare or twenty times that twenty.

Cap would have signed away every last penny he had and all his hope of gaining more if only he could see those three murderers dangle at the end of a hangman's rope.

With that prospect in mind he sat back in agreeable, if not exactly contented, silence and did not fuss or growl any more the rest of the way into Virginia City.

Chapter Twenty-seven

Cap had seen better saloons. But then he'd seen worse too. The place had a two-story high false front but only one floor's worth of plank walls once you got past the facade, and the roof was still nothing but canvas stretched across a framework made of aspen poles. Apparently The Glory Hole was growing at a cautious rate of speed, no doubt because gold camps like this one had a reputation for blossoming quick as a cactus flower after a summer rain, but fading away just as suddenly.

True to his word, the freighter Simms took Cap inside and introduced him to a man who looked entirely too young to be master of his own place.

"Barney Smith, I'd like you to meet a fellow with a story you might ought to listen to. I thought you might wanta help him when you hear why he's here. Barney, this is . . . come to think of it, mister, I don't recall getting your name."

"Marsden. You can call me Cap," he said, extending his hand to the blond-haired boy in sleeve garters. He was young, barely into his twenties, Cap guessed, but tall. He towered a head and a half above Cap's rather ordinary and uninspiring height.

An expression of polite boredom quickened into a huge smile at Cap's words. "Marsden, you said? *Captain* Marsden?"

"Not in the war, son. Don't misunderstand."

"No, sir, not . . . you're really Captain Marsden? Uh, um, oh what the hell was it . . . Alden? Alton? Alvin, that was it. You're Captain Alvin Marsden?"

"Now however would a boy your age come to know that?" Cap returned, completely puzzled.

Young Smith grinned. "You headed a company of free trappers out into the Englishmen's country. That would've been the fall of '35? or was it '36?"

"Eighteen hundred and thirty-six, that would've been," Cap told him. "Cold winter that year but the weather wasn't half as cold as the reception we got by the Britishers out in the Oregon country. They stole everything we owned, just about." Cap laughed. "Then we turned around and stole it all back and then some for good measure. But how would a boy like you know about those times?"

"My grampap told me, sir. Lordy, I grew up listening to his stories."

"Your grampa?"

"He was in your brigade that season, Captain. Tyndal Smith, his name was. D'you recollect him?"

"Tincup Smith? I hope to say that I do." Cap shook his head. "I haven't seen nor heard anything about Tincup since . . ." he shook his head again, "I can't remember when. It's been that long ago."

"Grampap quit the mountains two seasons after your run-ins with the Hudson's Bay boys. He'd had a good season for himself, him and a man name of Winslow Walker trapping together, just the two of them. Grampap had some money in his pocket and decided to cash in while he still had his hair. He came home to Missoura and the farm. My folks still live there."

"Tincup had a wife and family back in the States? I never knew that." There was no point in mentioning that Tincup also had a wife and runny-nosed family down in the Crow country nor the Snake woman he'd carried along for their winter in Oregon.

"Well we all sure knew everything about you and the other fellows Grampap trapped with. He was proud of his time in the mountains. He talked about it all the time. Always wondered what happened to you though, and to Walker and some of the others."

"Winslow went under . . . it must have been the summer after your grampa and him split the blanket. I know he'd done pretty well by himself. In the South Park country that was, I think. The Bayou Salade."

"That's right. They trapped the creeks in South Park, then legged it up into High Park before the Utes came up off the grasslands so they could wait out the winter there. They had a fine catch that year and sold out their plews to Sublette and that bunch. You say Walker was killed?"

"Uh-huh. If I remember right, Winslow and a man name of Brown—him I don't remember so well, he was a greenhorn new to the mountains and why Winslow took him under wing I'll never know—the two of them decided to go back south. I was putting up a bunch to go north and west again. That's where the best beaver was at the time, but Walker'd had such a good season with your grandad that he wanted to go south again. I heard—this was years after so I'm not real sure about any of it—but I heard they ran into a party of Cheyenne somewhere along the Arkansas. No idea what they'd have been doing out where Cheyenne could come on them, but that's what I heard. Heard they made a respectable fight of it before they went under, though. A man could do worse."

"Grampap never knew that," young Smith said.

"How is your grandfather now?"

"He died three years ago this past spring. He went easy though, surrounded by family and with time to make peace with his maker. He knew it was coming. He told me he hadn't any regrets, not a one."

"I'm sorry he's gone," Cap said. "I would have enjoyed seeing old Tincup again."

"He sure admired you, sir. Talked about you an awful lot."

"It's nice of you to say so, son."

"Captain, sir, Mr. Simms says there may be some way I can help you. I can promise you one thing for sure. If there's anything I can do for you, now or anytime else, I'll be really proud to do it."

"Now that's mighty nice of you, son. But I'll give you fair warning. I'm going to take you up on that offer."

"It will be my pleasure, sir."

"Cap. Just call me Cap."

Chapter Twenty-eight

"Good morning, captain, sir."

Cap had given up trying to get young Barney Smith to refer to him in a less formal manner. The boy simply couldn't do it. Which, Cap reflected, spoke well of his upbringing. Respect for his elders was too much a part of him to be ignored now, and perhaps especially so when most of his early life he'd been subjected to Tincup's windies. There was little doubt in Cap's mind that his old friend Tyndal Smith would have gilded the lily more than a little when spinning tall tales for his grandchildren. But then that sort of thing was forgivable.

"Good morning, Barney." Cap yawned and rubbed at his face with both hands. He'd gotten late to bed and was feeling it this morning. Sand lay by the bucketful in the corners of his eyes, or so it felt.

"Care for an eye-opener this morning?"

Cap grimaced. He enjoyed a dram now and then. But the idea was not so appealing at . . . what was it? Six in the morning? Something like that. Even if the whiskey would help to wash some of the fur off his tongue, he did not think his stomach was quite up to it yet. He shook his head. "You wouldn't have some food around, would you, son?"

"No, sorry. Cold stuff left over from the free lunch, that's all."

The thought of pickled pigs feet and hard crackers for breakfast was no more palatable than the whiskey would have been. "I'll pass, thank you."

Smith, Cap noticed, had been up even later last night than he, but looked bright-eyed and full of vinegar already at this hour. Seemed to be able to stomach his whiskey already too. Youth. There were advantages to it that a man didn't particularly think about until he no longer had it.

"There's a cafe the next street over and a block and a half down," Smith offered. "They serve a pretty good meal there if you aren't looking for anything fancy."

"I expect I can make do without fancy if I have to," Cap told him with a grin.

"Yes, sir. So Grampap always told me. Is it true you trappers used to eat mountain lion?"

"Painter cats? Lordy, son, that's the best-tasting meat there is. Better than boudins, better than tongue, even better than elk. And elk meat is hard to beat."

"I always thought maybe Grampap was pulling my leg about that one."

"No, sir. Do you ever get the chance, try it. You'll see. Your grampa was a truthful man." Which was probably a lie in itself, but no harm done.

"Well, you won't find any lion meat on the menu at Louis's cafe, but the prices are fair and his missus makes biscuits so light they have to serve them with a towel laid over, lest they float right off the plate."

Cap laughed. "I can see, son, that you're every bit

as honest and truthful a man as your grampa."
Which brought a chuckle from Smith.

"By the way, sir, I put the word out last night to
everyone who came in. If the men you're looking
for are anywhere around Virginia City, I'll hear
back about it. This is a hard camp, and a man is
pretty much free to be as rough as he can stand up
to, but we don't take to the sort that would harm a
child the way those men did to your granddaughter.
None of the boys here would put up with such as
that."

"I appreciate that, son. Thanks."

"It's the least I could do for Old Mar—I mean, for
Captain Alvin Marsden."

Cap laughed again. "It's all right, Barney. I've
been called Old Marsden since I wasn't much older
than you. To us free trappers it was meant to be
respectful of a man's experience. Didn't have aught
to do with his age."

"Yes, sir, I knew that. But it sounds so . . . you
know."

"It's all right, Barney. Really. And I'd be proud for
you to call me Old Marsden. Makes me feel kind of
to home out here in the far country again."

Barney grinned. "Yes, sir. I'll do that," he said.
Although Cap couldn't help but notice that in fact
he did not do it. Couldn't bring himself to quite yet,
Cap supposed.

"You say the cafe is a street over and a little ways
down?"

"Want me to show you, sir?"

Cap shook his head. "No need. Just point me
which way it is. I expect I can find it on my own."

Chapter Twenty-nine

The big question of the morning was, Where was that darn cafe? The directions were simple enough, so where did he go wrong?

It occurred to Cap that here he was, lost in a town that was no bigger than the temporary crowds they'd assembled at the old rendezvous sites back in the shining times. Lost and confused by a few silly streets and blocks, and him a man who could find his way across mountains and prairies where no whites had ever traveled before, much less mapped or laid out into dinky little squares.

It was amazing.

Useful too, though. He spotted a striped barber pole on the far side of the street and fingered his chin, which was matted with whiskers grown long enough to turn soft. He needed a shave. Having a beard was fine. He'd sometimes gone a dozen years or more between opportunities to see his own face in a mirror. But after so long a spell of shaving, he was finding this new growth prickly and too, too itchy, especially on his throat and under his chin. The rest of it wasn't so bad, but the itching at his throat was like to drive him crazy if he didn't get some relief from it. That would happen one of two ways. He could get it shaved off now or he could suffer through until the itching quit of its own accord. He decided he'd get a shave right after breakfast. He was gray enough without flaunting a snowy white beard to make it all the worse.

Cap yawned and considered asking for fresh directions to the cafe Barney'd said should be somewhere along this street. Maybe there was no sign? Barney hadn't exactly specified what the place looked like.

A man stepped out of an alley a little way ahead. Cap thought about asking him. It was a trifle embarrassing to accost strangers with dumb questions, darn it. But he was hungry. He altered his course slightly so as to approach the man, who had stopped and was standing there staring at Cap.

"Mind if I ask you something?" Cap called out when he was a dozen paces distant.

"You!" the fellow blurted. "You're the son of a bitch."

The response seemed a mite excessive for such a simple request. Cap thought to explain himself, but the man didn't give him time. The fellow reached into a coat pocket and pulled out a stubby, squat little pepperbox pistol.

"Now look a-here," Cap said, "you must have me confused with someone else. All I want is—"

"You're the son of a bitch that's been spreading lies about us," the man shouted.

He raised his pistol and took aim.

Cap thought about going for the tomahawk in his belt. His rifle was back at Barney Smith's saloon, left standing in a corner of the room the boy had given for Cap's use.

There'd been a time when Cap Marsden would not have so much as considered stepping away from the campfire to pick up some forest litter to use for a fire without taking his rifle in hand.

But those days were a long time past, and years of city living had taken the habits of hair-saving caution away from him.

Now this stranger on a Virginia City street was aiming a revolving pistol at him for no reason, none at all.

"Wait a minute," Cap protested. "Just hold on there."

The pistol spat, the sound of it light and faintly hollow. A flash of yellow fire blossomed at the front of the boxy thing, and a halo of pale smoke surrounded it. Cap heard the ball sizzle past his ear with a sound like a hornet's rapid drone.

"Wait, I said, I—"

The man fired again. Missed again too. If he kept this up . . .

Cap reached for the hand ax at his belt. He had his tomahawk and the butcher knife, but at any distance greater than belly to belly, only the tomahawk was worth trying. A kitchen knife can be a formidable enough weapon, but they aren't balanced to throw, and only a fool would try it. The tomahawk, however, would work fine from a distance. Up to a point. Cap had to get closer if he expected the hatchet to spin full circle and properly connect with the blade facing forward and the weight of the shaft driving it home into bone and flesh.

He didn't need time to think all that through. The old habits had been buried, but they hadn't been destroyed. He swept the tomahawk from his belt.

Someone, something poked him in the upper

arm. It felt like a light punch, as if a ten-year-old boy had reared back and let his fist fly. The impact was neither especially hard nor particularly painful.

Funny thing, though, Cap's whole arm and right hand went numb. The tomahawk, too heavy for him to grasp, slipped from his suddenly weak fingers.

Someone or something else punched him again, this time in the lower back on his left side.

In front of him the man in the street fired the pistol a third time, and this time either his aim or his luck had improved, because Cap saw the fire and almost instantly felt the sting of a small-caliber bullet smacking him in the upper left part of his chest, squarely where a man's heart is said to be.

Cap felt a chill of fear then for the first time. He felt . . .

More gunshots. He heard two more gunshots, coming virtually simultaneously. But from behind, both of them. One of the bullets must have missed, or at least he did not feel its impact. The other he was sure of. It struck him in the left hip and spun him half around, that leg going as numb as his arm already was.

He heard more shots. Rather dimly felt more bullets find him.

No, he thought with a detached calm, it wasn't so much that he could feel those shots. It was that he heard them. He heard the damp, dull thump of the lead pellets burying themselves in living meat. One, two, four more? He was no longer sure how many times he'd been hit.

He was not sure of very much right now, actually.

He seemed to be lying on the ground. He didn't remember falling, but he could smell the rich, yeasty scent of soil and could feel the lightly stinging bite of gravel on his cheek.

It was hard for him to see. His vision was blurry, with a thin haze obscuring the images before him. The strongest impression was of a yellowish brown. It was the color of the bare, sun-baked street, he thought. Beyond that he was not certain.

There were a few more sounds. Dull reports that might have been more gunshots. Distant shouting. A crackling, bubbling wheeze that Cap suspected was the sound of his own breathing loud in his ears.

It was . . .

Oh, God. It hurt. A wave of sharp, shocking pain shot through him like a bolt of lightning, and he felt his body tense against the onslaught.

Until then it had all been indistinct and free from pain. But not this jolt. It seared through him, seeking out every nerve end in his body, or so it felt, and giving it a yank and a twist for good measure.

God!

And then it did not hurt any longer. A blackness drove through him, and all sensation was taken away.

Chapter Thirty

It hurt. God, it hurt. Pain was everywhere. The pain filled him, twisted and turned inside him beyond his ability to stand it. He couldn't stand it. But he couldn't make it stop.

He screamed. He was not sure any sound came out, but he screamed. The pain. Oh, the pain.

It proved he was alive. That was not necessarily a good thing. If this was the alternative, then he would welcome death. At least that would stop the pain. Stop the pain. Please, God, stop the pain.

Cap stiffened. Cried out again. Then, subsiding, he sank back into blackness, welcoming the relief that came to him.

He was out of his mind. He understood that in a vague sort of way. A thin and tenuous link with consciousness was there, but he could not trust it. He was imagining things. Margaret's voice. He could hear Margaret's voice, not calling out to him, not summoning him to or from the grave, but really quite ordinary, chatting bright and cheerful as he remembered from . . . when? He did not know. Before Rebecca was torn from them. That long ago.

Now the pain was less than it had been, but his mind was affected. He knew that because he heard Margaret's voice.

It occurred to him to marvel that it would be his daughter's voice he heard now on his deathbed and not that of his own beloved and departed Becca. He'd rather hoped Becca would be there to meet him when his time came, but apparently that was not to be. He sighed, and the flow of Margaret's talking changed.

"Poppa? Are you awake, Poppa? Are you?"

She sounded so real to him that he almost responded. Then he remembered in time that it was all but a dream, an imagining and not real. Real was . . . pain, that's what real was. Not quite so completely filling now, not so thoroughly choking away all other senses. But pain, yes, it remained. Above and through and beyond all else there was the pain. He wished Margaret would let him go, wished Becca would come to welcome him into whatever mystery lay on the other side of the line that we know as life.

Not quite yet, though. Not quite.

Cap let himself drift back into the blackness where the pain could not reach him.

"Ahhhhh!" Pain ripped through him. Stabbed deep and twisted. Cap stiffened against its onslaught and tried to brace himself against it. His eyes snapped open, staring, straining for a vision of . . . what? He did not know.

Whatever he expected to see, it was not to be. But what he did see made him blink and doubt his own sanity.

Margaret, pale and worried. "Poppa?"

Cap's lips trembled as he tried to remember how to speak. It took him a moment. Then, his own voice a dry and scarcely recognizable sound that was harsh in his ears, he whispered, "Wh . . . whe . . . ?" He wanted to ask where Becca was, why it was Margaret who was here, but he could not get it out.

Margaret, misunderstanding his meaning, came forward to lean over him, her expression a mask of deep worry. She bent closer and he felt the touch of a cool, damp cloth on his forehead and over his cheeks. The feeling was marvelous. Refreshing. And . . . real.

"I'm here, Poppa. Three days now. Your . . . the accident was weeks ago. A man named Smith sent word. Cathy and I took the next steamer upriver. George sent a man with us to look after us. He had to stay in Omaha, you see. We . . . Rebecca was buried there. We couldn't wait for you, Poppa. We had to take care of her without you. I hope you understand."

Cap could see tears glistening bright on Margaret's cheeks in the light of a lamp he hadn't noticed before. The room he was in, wherever it was, smelled of carbolic and camphor and other strong, stinking odors he could not begin to identify.

He was alive, he concluded. Be damned if he wasn't. It came as something of a surprise to him. Likely was going to surprise some others too.

"Where?" he managed, his voice a thin croak.

"Where was Rebecca buried? In Omaha, of course, Poppa. In the Protestant cemetery there."

Cap shook his head, the movement setting off a renewed spate of sharp pain that made him stiffen against the mattress he was lying on. He grimaced and sucked in his breath.

"Poppa. Are you all right?"

He smiled at that. He couldn't help himself. Slowly, with great care, lest he move again and set off the pain once more, he whispered, "Stupid question, child."

Margaret blinked and for a moment looked ready to cry, she was so taken aback by her father's comment. Then, despite the depth of her worry, she began to laugh. "Yes, it was, wasn't it?"

Cap did not laugh. Lord, he wouldn't dare jostle and jog himself like that or the pain would rip him in two. But he managed a grim smile. "That's my girl."

Margaret became serious again. She wiped his face with the moist cloth and clucked a little. "Are you going to be all right, Poppa? Are you going to live?"

He thought about the question for a few seconds before he tried to answer her.

He hadn't been at all sure that he would. And even less sure that he wanted to.

But . . . he weighed the implications of the choices . . . yes, yes, dammit, he was.

Rebecca. Little Rebecca was in the ground now. And having just lost her elder daughter, now Margaret was filled with dread at the thought of losing her father too.

Well, she was not going to see that happen. Not yet. Not while the men who'd murdered Rebecca were still alive to walk the face of this earth.

Those sons of bitches would not be allowed to kill two members of this family. They would not.

Cap looked into Margaret's eyes for a moment. Then, carefully, he whispered, "I'm going to be just fine."

Then he closed his eyes and embraced the healing blackness once again.

Chapter Thirty-one

"They tell me you're going to live." Tincup's grandson smiled down at him.

"Looking like it," Cap agreed. He still hurt like hell, but at this point he was willing to go on living. That was something, anyway. "I'm told you're the biggest reason I'm still alive."

Smith shook his head. "The reason you're still alive, sir, is that you're too damn tough to die. We don't have a regular doctor here, but the barber says you should've been dead. You were shot at least eight times. The worst of it was in your lung. He didn't think you could make it through after that, but you did. Grampa was an awfully tough old man too, though. I guess it took tough men to do what you and he used to."

"The barber. I recall it was right outside his shop where I ran into that fellow."

"That's right. It helped, I'm sure, that he was right there, Johnny-on-the-spot to stop the bleeding."

"And I wasn't shot in the heart? Sure did think he'd hit me there."

Smith smiled again. "I thought so too when I saw you. He tells me that a man's heart isn't so much on the left side as it's pretty much in the middle. Just kind of tilted a mite to the left. I don't know why everybody insists on thinking of it off to the left so far, but I did too until he told me different. If Shear hadn't thought so along with all the rest of us, I suppose he would have shot you through the heart, and we wouldn't be having this talk now."

"Shear," Cap said. "He was the one that shot me down?"

"You didn't know?"

Cap managed to shake his head without the small movement resulting in very much pain at all. It was a considerable improvement over the way things had been. "I saw him. Didn't know him. There was others too? I seem t'recall balls coming at me from someplace else too."

"Shear was the one in front of you. His friends, Tom Rayne and Art Coffrey, snuck up behind. It was deliberate, of course. There were plenty of witnesses. They must have seen you on the street and sent Shear into the alley to wait for you to approach while the others hung back out of sight until you walked by. They weren't taking any chances."

"Bold sons of bitches, aren't they?" Cap mused. "All three of them were there?"

Smith nodded.

"I never saw but the one." He sighed. "Coffrey, the third man's name is. That'd be the one they call Coffee, of course." He grunted. "Nice to know his name finally, though it seems on the hard side of things to go about learning it this particular way."

"In a way I feel that it's my fault," Barney Smith told him. "If I hadn't broadcast the fact that you wanted those men, and for what, they wouldn't have known anyone was after them. They wouldn't have been on their guard, wouldn't have known there was any danger for them here."

"I don't s'pose . . ."

Smith shook his head. "They weren't caught, of course. We don't have much in the way of law around here to begin with. If they'd stayed and there was time for the word to spread about what they did—not to you particularly but to a little girl—they would've been grabbed and hanged sure enough. But it takes awhile for a town to work itself up to a lynching. I guess they knew that and didn't want to have to worry about finding you behind them someday. Still hunting them and able to do something about it. They saw you, sprang their trap, and then hightailed it out of town before justice could be served. I'm sorry, sir. Very sorry."

"Not your fault, son." He grinned a little. "And their bad luck that I lived."

"I . . . I suppose you've been told."

"Told?"

"Sir. Captain Marsden."

"Yes?"

"You . . . sound like you still want to go after those men."

"Damn right I do."

"Sir, I . . . I suppose Mrs. Brenn hasn't been able to bring herself to tell you. And Ben . . . he's our barber and part-time doctor, Ben Dantzle . . . I don't think you've ever seen him. While you're awake, I mean."

"No, I haven't," Cap agreed.

"Yes, sir, well . . . the thing is, sir . . . I mean . . ."

"Just say it, son. Whatever it is, you act like it's something I ought to know."

"Yes, sir. I . . . Captain Marsden, sir, Ben tells us that one of those pistol balls struck you in the hip. It broke the joint there, the ball that moves inside a socket. That's the way he explained it."

"I've seen bones before. I know where he means. What of it?" Cap asked.

"Sir, I'm awful sorry to tell you this, but . . . you won't ever be able to walk again."

Chapter Thirty-two

The trip back down the Missouri to Omaha was without question the worst time in Cap's long and not always easy life.

And the pain was the least of it, although that was plenty bad enough.

First jostled, tossed, and constantly thumped by the harsh, virtually unsprung motions of a wagon just to reach the river landing, he arrived at the steamboat wharf barely alive.

Several of his wounds were torn open by the rough treatment in the wagon, and it was all Margaret could do to stanch the many wounds on Cap's lean and wrinkled old body.

Almost as unpleasant as the pain and the bleeding was the old man's embarrassment to be seen so intimately and as such a weakling by his own daughter.

There had been a time when a much younger man had learned—reluctantly—to change an infant's diapers.

Now the heat rose fierce and burning into his cheeks and he held his eyes clamped hard closed when she had to do very much the same service for him.

Pain, though, and embarrassment were only the beginnings of his discomfort.

Never to walk again?

The thought of it was beyond bearing.

Once, on his first venture far from the restraints and the security of civilized society, a very young Alvin Marsden had found himself alone in an unknown wilderness with neither horse nor weapons nor material comforts, save for the clothes on his back and a belt knife.

He'd been too brash and ignorant to be properly frightened at the time, merely took his belt up a notch and walked south until he came to water, then followed the banks of the North Platte until he found sign of other whites and followed them until he caught up with Beckworth and the rest of the bunch. His own companions had long since abandoned him, thinking him dead and scalped.

Cap had hiked, he later guessed, three hundred fifty miles through territory that was unknown to him.

He hadn't been afraid for one moment of that time.

Now he was afraid.

Now he was terrified.

Never to walk again? To spend the remainder of his time on earth having to rely on others to wait on him? Carry for him? Dress and clean him?

He would rather die than live like that.

Better to take a pistol and send a ball through his own brain, he believed, than accept the cruelty of continued life so completely crippled.

Better to go out a man, with a man's ability to

cope and choose, than to become a constant burden to his own children.

The trip back to Omaha was a bitter draught to drink.

Chapter Thirty-three

Margaret gave him a smile when she walked into the ground-floor room they'd fixed up as his. It was the same smile she always showed him, broad and cheery and so perky it made him want to puke. If it had been any more brittle, her face would have busted, any more phony and it would have smelled like a dead trout. Cap wondered if she thought she was fooling him with all these insipid, stupid, insulting grins.

But then maybe it was herself she was trying to fool into believing that all would yet be well, and not him at all. Cap's heart turned over inside his chest and gave a small lurch.

Poor Margaret. Poor, dear Margaret. She'd lost her elder child and now she was standing watch over a crippled and useless father who she likely thought would become a permanent burden to her.

Well, that wasn't going to happen. Cap had thought it through, and knew that much for certain.

He would *not* become a drain on the emotions of his children. Not Margaret here, nor Donald downriver in St. Louis, nor little—huh, she was, what, twenty-six years old now—Lillian out in San Francisco.

The point was, he had no intention of saddling any or all of them with his care for years and years and unending years to come.

No, sir. He still had something to say about it. And so he would when the time came.

"Good morning, Poppa," Margaret said in a heartily perky voice that was as faked-up and phony as her never-ending smile. "How are we today?"

"We," Cap said, bearing down with deliberate sarcasm on the word, "want to go home."

"Now, Poppa, you know we can't let you do that. Who would take care of you? No, please, George and I have talked this over. We want you to stay here with us. It's all decided, really. And just wait until you see what we've done. Just wait."

Cap sniffed. "What've you been up to this time? Does it have anything to do with all that pounding and hammering yesterday? I couldn't get my afternoon nap for all that, you know. Kept me awake the whole day long."

"I know," Margaret admitted. "But you'll like it when you see. I know you will."

Cap sniffed again, more of a snort than a sniff really, to show his disbelief.

He heard some shuffling and whispering outside his door, and Margaret's insufferable grin became even more syrupy sweet. Which he would not have thought possible if he hadn't seen it for himself.

"Close your eyes, Poppa."

Cap grimaced. "Don't want to close my eyes," he grumbled.

"Please, Poppa. For me."

He hesitated for a bit, just to show that he dang well didn't have to do what anybody else wanted, then he shut his eyes.

He heard more faint sounds that he could not identify, and then a giggle that he knew was Cathy, and a solid, heavy footstep that told him George was there too, although why George should be here and not at work was a mystery. Poor George. In a way Cap felt sorriest for George. At least with Margaret and Catherine, Cap was blood family. To George he was just an old man, and a crippled and burdensome one at that. Poor George. Poor Margaret. Poor all of them. Cap growled a little and opened his eyes without waiting to be told it was all right to do so.

What he saw surprised him, all right.

It was a chair. Tall. With a wicker seat and padded back.

The crazy thing was that the chair was riding on wheels. Great big wheels in back and a pair of tiny little wheels in the front. The little wheels were mounted on casters so that they could swivel and turn about.

A handsome lap robe was laid out on the seat of the chair, and there were handles at the back of it so someone could grab hold there. Or use them to push with and steer the ugly contraption, Cap saw immediately.

"Ta-da!" Cathy said with a bright, childish laugh that was one of the few genuine expressions Cap had heard since they'd carried him down the Big Muddy and off the steamer.

There was a man Cap did not know standing behind the wheeled chair. A huge man, black as anthracite coal and big as a buffalo's front end.

"Poppa Marsden," George announced, "this is Cleofus Brown. He will be spending days with you from now on, and between Cleofus and this chair you will be able to get up and go wherever you want. You won't have to worry about being a nuisance to Margaret. Which I know you've been worrying about." George grinned, proud of himself for coming up with this solution to Cap's miseries. Well, a solution for Margaret's miseries was really more like it, which Cap understood and did not in the least resent. And in truth, if this ugly contraption would take some of the burden off Margaret, well, that was all right.

Cap did not want to seem too eager to accept the situation though. He scowled and grunted and looked Cleofus over from toe to head and back again.

The man was huge, with bulging muscles and skin so healthy it looked oiled.

"Bought me my own personal nigger, did you, George?" Cap said in a loudly rude voice. The big man behind the wheelchair never changed expression.

"That . . . isn't the way I would have put it, Poppa Marsden."

"Not while he could overhear anyway," Cap said.

"If you don't want—"

"No, this is a good idea. I admit it. A fine idea. Get me outta the house and out from underfoot." Cap cocked his head and squinted up at the stoic black man. "You want to take me out for a trial run in that thing, Cleofus Brown?"

Brown didn't answer. He nodded and came around the wheelchair to the side of the bed, bent, and lifted Cap off the bed as if he weighed no more than a banty rooster. Margaret took the lap robe and shook it out, and Brown deposited Cap onto the chair, leaned down, and carefully arranged the old man's legs onto a small shelf set low to the ground. Then, with Cathy's help, Margaret spread the robe over Cap's lap and legs, straightening and tucking the thick wool until it was all to her liking.

"How does that feel, Poppa?"

"I don't know yet." Cap craned his neck around to look back toward Brown. "Can you make this thing keep up with a horse, Cleofus Brown?"

"Yes, suh," Brown said meekly, his voice a deep bass rumble that rose from his chest. "If that's what you tell me to do, suh."

"Uh-huh. Well I tell you what, Cleofus Brown. Let's you and me go see some of the sights of Omaha, shall we?"

Brown did not say anything, merely bobbed his head and took hold of the handles at the back of the chair.

"If we aren't back in time for dinner, don't wait for me," Cap said. "I have business to tend to."

"Poppa, don't you think . . . ?"

Cap didn't wait for Margaret to finish protesting the announcement. He snapped his fingers imperiously and motioned for Brown to wheel him out the door and toward what was intended to be a sort of relative freedom.

Chapter Thirty-four

Cap waited until they were out on the street, well away from the cloying presence of Margaret and her worries, before he spoke again. "First thing, Mr. Brown, is I want to apologize to you."

Brown said nothing, but continued to push the wheelchair along the side of the rutted street. The chair bounced as bad as a wagon did, Cap was finding, and that hurt like hell. Not that there was any point in complaining about it. Whining, he'd found out long ago, accomplished almighty little other than annoying those who had to listen to it.

"Stop here a minute, please."

The chair came to a halt.

"Step around here to where I can see you, please."

Brown did as he was asked, but his eyes were carefully averted, inspecting something in the general direction of his shoes.

"Like I said, Mr. Brown, I want to apologize. What I was doing back there was trying to judge what sort of man you are."

Brown might have been carved out of pumice, for all the response he gave.

"I used that ugly term deliberate," Cap said. "To tell you the truth, I'd've had more respect for you if you'd hauled off and socked me, or spit in my face. You didn't, but that isn't to your credit."

Brown looked at him now, his expression surly.

"Good," Cap declared. "You're paying attention. I want you to understand something. When I first left the States, there was slaves back east. Just about every man of color, or woman, was property. Reckon I don't have to tell you about that. I expect somebody owned you too."

Brown did not answer. But then he did not have to. The odds were long against him having been one of the few Negroes to receive emancipation before the issue was forced.

"Out here, Cleofus Brown, there wasn't any such thing as slavery. Out in the mountains amongst the free trappers and the fur traders, the only way a man was judged was by what he could do. Nobody cared what he looked like. One of my best friends was a man named Beckworth. You ever hear of him?"

Brown did not answer, which Cap took to mean he did not know about Beckworth.

"He was a friend of mine, and many a time we've shared liquor, blankets, tobacco, and even women." Cap smiled a little and added, "Though I would appreciate it if you wouldn't mention that to my daughter. I don't think she would cotton to that too well. Anyway, the point is, my friend Jim was colored. Not as dark as you, but he was black as night. He used to tease the rest of us that he always felt safe around us at night because any Injuns sneaking up on us would be sure to spot us before him and he could get away from them clean while they were busy putting us under. He was a good man, Beckworth. A man to trust.

"And I guess what I'm saying here, apart from saying I'm sorry that I went and deliberately offended you like that, is that I hope you are as good and trustworthy a man as Jim Beckworth was. Now if you don't mind, I'd like to start this partnership over, because I'm hoping I can lean on you for some favors this next little while. Things I won't want George or my daughter to know about. And to start off with, my friends generally call me Cap. Or Old Marsden. That would do. As for you, you might tell me what you're called."

Brown remained mute.

After a moment, when it was obvious that he did not intend to speak further, Cap said, "All right. You see no reason to trust me. That's fair enough after what I did. Please take me to a gunsmith, Mr. Brown, or to a hardware that stocks firearms. I have some purchases to make."

Silently, Brown moved again to the back of the chair and began to push Cap along the street.

Chapter Thirty-five

The smith was a man named Pryce. He was thin and wiry and smelled faintly of solvents, solder, and bluing agents. He had enough hair growing out of his nostrils for it to be worthwhile harvesting and spinning it into yarn. The look he gave to Cap and to Brown was one of suspicion. Cap suspected Pryce was a man more comfortable with tools than with people. Which was just fine by Cap, so long as the man knew his trade.

"I want a revolver," Cap told him. "Cartridge revolver." Cap neither liked nor much respected short arms. But if a man was going to mess with one, it might as well be the best that was available. "Accurate. Large-caliber."

"Smith & Wesson makes the only revolvers on the market with self-contained cartridges for ammunition," Pryce told him. "They're the only ones that have the right, something to do with patent protections, but I wouldn't call any of them large-caliber. Mostly they produce weapons in .32 rimfire. Their catalog offers a .38 caliber model, but I've never seen either the gun or the cartridges in that size. Would a .32 be large enough for you?"

"It would not. I want a .44, ideally the same rimfire cartridge that I use in my rifle. Something big enough to have some authority to it."

Cap figured he was living proof that the lead slugs from small cartridges were not always lethal. It had been small-caliber slugs that Coffrey and company had shot him full of back in Virginia City. Cap had survived a large number of hits then. A .44, he believed, would eliminate the possibility of a repeat performance.

"Sorry," the gunsmith told him. "I have plenty of revolvers in .44 caliber, but they all load loose powder and ball. Of course, you can buy paper cartridges for those. They aren't as slow to load as using a flask and pouch."

Cap shook his head stubbornly. "No, it's a cartridge weapon that I want. I'm told the big cap-and-ball revolvers can be modified to accept self-contained ammunition. You drill out the cylinder, remove the ram, and add a loading gate at the back, and there you have it. Or so I've been told. I know a man in Santa Fe that does it. I'd go to him, except that I don't happen to be in Santa Fe."

"There are laws about making those guns, mister. Smith & Wesson could sue me for patent infringement if I did what you want. It's a wonder they haven't already sued your friend in Santa Fe."

"Do you really think Smith & Wesson is going to care what one gunsmith in Omaha does? I know for a fact they haven't bothered with the fellow down south. They wouldn't bother suing you either."

"I don't know that they would or they wouldn't, do I? Can you think of a reason why I should risk

Frank Roderus

a lawsuit just so you can have what you want, mister?"

Cap gave the man a slow looking-over, then said, "I'll buy the revolver from you, pay for your work to convert it, buy a case of ammunition to fit it, and pay you a bonus of a hundred dollars. And if it makes you feel any better, I'll promise not to tell the Smith & Wesson Company about you."

"A hundred dollars?"

"Gold coin in the hand," Cap affirmed.

"Two hundred," Pryce countered.

"A hundred fifty."

"Done."

"For that price, mister, I'll want a good job done. And a quick one."

"Pick out the gun you want me to modify, mister. I'll start on it right here and now. I, uh, have had my best success with the Remington. It's a stronger frame than the Colt, takes to the conversion better, don't you see."

"You've done this before, then."

"I didn't say that, did I? Not in so many words."

"When will my gun be ready?"

"Would Friday afternoon be soon enough?"

Cap nodded. "We'll be back Friday afternoon." Cap pulled a twenty-dollar gold piece from his pocket and laid it on the counter. "I'll have the rest for you on Friday."

"If you expect to have the gun you will," Pryce said.

Cap decided he did not particularly like Gunsmith Pryce.

But then it wasn't the man's personality that was important here. Just the quality of his work.

"Take me to the telegraph office next, please, Mr. Brown," Cap said to his silent companion once they were outdoors. "And then I'll be wanting a good carpenter, if you happen to know one."

"I know a black man who makes coffins," Brown grudgingly said.

"Perfect," Cap told him. "We'll see him right after the telegraph office."

"Yes, suh." Brown gave Cap's chair a stiff push and started the old man bumping and bouncing down the street again.

Chapter Thirty-six

Cap leaned forward to retrieve a chicken leg from the platter, and was pleased to note that the movement cost him very little in the way of pain. Most of his wounds were as good as healed now. Except of course for the hip. They told him that would never be right again.

Still, it was something of a relief to be able to come to the table with Margaret and her family again. It had been too awkward before, and too embarrassing, having to be lifted and carried anywhere he wanted to go. Now, in the wheeled chair George had gotten for him, he was able to get around at a very nearly normal level of activity.

More or less.

The thing that bothered Cap the most now, though, had nothing to do with either his own lack of mobility nor the continued pain his wounds brought to him. It was instead the empty chair at Cathy's side. The chair Rebecca should have occupied.

Cap had been spared that during the weeks he'd spent confined to a sickbed. The others had had to face the ugly fact daily through all that time. No one spoke about it openly. In fact, none of them mentioned Rebecca's name out loud. It was almost as if they believed, or hoped, that the pain of her death could be diminished if the pain, and the child, were ignored hereafter. Cap did not know that that was necessarily true. He rather suspected that tucking anguish out of sight does nothing to diminish it, but only makes one bear it alone.

He looked at Rebecca's place, nothing but bare polished wood where she should have been, and cleared his throat as if to speak. Then he decided otherwise. He would give them time. Perhaps Margaret, George, and Cathy should be allowed their own schedule for grieving. Cap certainly had demanded his own as to manner and method—and look what that had gained him—but surely they should be permitted the same privilege as he had claimed for himself.

He settled for the chicken leg and a second helping of mashed potatoes.

"George."

"Yes, Poppa Marsden?"

"Have you heard anything back from your wires?"

George glanced first at his wife and then at little Cathy, as if in apology, before he answered. "No, Poppa Marsden."

"Nothing from the authorities? Nothing from Barney Smith either?"

George shook his head. "I'm sorry."

George had blanketed the entire west, everywhere from Omaha to San Francisco, with telegraph inquiries about the three men Cap was able to name and describe for him. That had been weeks ago, though, and no one admitted to having seen the men. Not since the day they shot Cap down in a quiet Virginia City street. The men had disappeared from Virginia City that morning and, for all intents and purposes, dropped off the face of the earth as well.

"You've sent wires to the police in Canada, George?" There was a good chance that men running from any point in the Montana or Idaho gold fields would dash north to put a border between themselves and any pursuit.

"Yes, Poppa Marsden, but I haven't heard anything from them either."

"And the railroad? You've sent notices all along the road?"

"Yes, and we asked the Central Pacific to do the same. They promised they would alert their people too. I . . . I think it is time for us all to put this aside, Poppa Marsden. Nothing we can do will change the past. Finding those men wouldn't bring our baby back to us. Finding them wouldn't make you walk again. I think it's time we stop thinking about them. After all, Poppa Marsden, vengeance belongs to the Lord, not to man."

Cap grunted. That was an easy enough thing for him to say. No, that wasn't fair to George or to Margaret. Putting tragedy behind was not at all an easy thing. Impossible sometimes. And it was not fair to judge them by his own standards. George, and for that matter Margaret too, knew only civil, law-abiding order in their safe and stable past lives. Their experiences were far from Cap's own.

"Ever read the Old Testament, George?"

"Not so much," his son-in-law admitted.

"Lots of blood there, George. Lots of killing."

"Meaning what, Poppa Marsden?"

"Meaning . . ." Cap sighed, "nothing much, I sup-

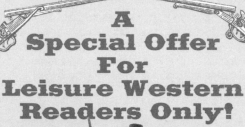

GET YOUR 4
FREE* BOOKS NOW—
A VALUE OF BETWEEN
$17 AND $20

Mail the Free* Books Certificate Today!

FREE* BOOKS
CERTIFICATE!

YES! I want to subscribe to the Leisure Western Book Club. Please send me my 4 FREE* BOOKS. Then, each month, I'll receive the four newest Leisure Western Selections to preview for 10 days. If I decide to keep them, I will pay the Special Member's Only discounted price of just $3.36 each, a total of $13.44 ($16.35 in Canada). This saves me between $3 and $6 off the bookstore price. There are no shipping, handling or other charges.* There is no minimum number of books I must buy and I may cancel the program at any time. In any case, the 4 FREE* BOOKS are mine to keep—at a value of between $17 and $20!

*In Canada, add $7.50 US shipping and handling per order for first shipment. For all subsequent shipments to Canada the cost of membership in the Book Club is $16.35 US plus $7.50 US shipping and handling per order. All payments must be made in US dollars.

Name _____

Address _____

City_____ State_____

Zip——————————— Telephone_____

Signature_____

Biggest Savings Offer!

For those of you who would like to pay us in advance by check or credit card—we've got an even bigger savings in mind. Interested? Check here. ☐

If under 18, parent or guardian must sign. Terms, prices and conditions subject to change. Subscription subject to acceptance. Leisure Books reserves the right to reject any order or cancel any subscription.

Tear here and mail your FREE* book card today!

Get Four Books Totally FREE* – A Value of between $16 and $20

Tear here and mail your FREE* book card today!

PLEASE RUSH
MY FOUR FREE*
BOOKS TO ME
RIGHT AWAY!

LeisureWestern Book Club
P.O. Box 6613
Edison, NJ 08818-6613

AFFIX
STAMP
HERE

pose." He changed the subject. "Where is Mr. Brown, George?"

"Out on the back stoop having his dinner, I think. Do you need him?"

"Not right away. After dinner will be fine."

"Would you like some green beans, Poppa?" Margaret asked.

"No, I . . . I think I've taken too much already." He looked at little Cathy, who had been silent throughout the meal. But then she rarely spoke lately. She never talked about her sister, but Cap thought the child was the one who was taking Rebecca's death the hardest. She no longer fluttered about asking questions. No longer laughed. Rarely even smiled. And she never, ever anymore asked her grandfather to tell her stories from his youth.

Something twisted and burned inside Cap's gut, but his expression did not change. He picked up the chicken leg and took a bite from it.

Chapter Thirty-seven

"Cap'n suh, I most generally tries to keep my mouth shut, but I got to tell you, suh, that there contraption is the awfullest thing I ever seen."

The carpenter, a lean man with generous streaks of gray in an otherwise bushy black beard, gave Cleofus Brown an angry look. "It's what the gennelmun ask me fo', Clee. I done what he want."

"And then some," Cap agreed, taking the odd-looking hickory implement from the coffee-with-cream-colored carpenter. He upended the object and peered at its tip. "What is this plate for?" he asked.

"I was thinkin', sir, the end there, it wears down if you use it much. So I had my friend make up that iron plate there. And see how it be screwed on? He made up another plate, this one here, with these here steel spikes stickin' down." The carpenter grinned, proud of himself for the innovation he'd come up with. "That way, do you want to walk in the winter, on the ice like, you don't slip an' fall down. I got that notion from the way they put the caulk on horseshoes in the wintertime, you know?"

"Very nice. I like it," Cap said. He turned the object right side up and examined the leather work. The thick, hard leather belt was padded all around with a generous layer of glove-soft kid that was stuffed with something, probably cotton batting. "I think this will work nicely."

The carpenter had gone to the trouble of staining and polishing the hickory so the curious getup was as nicely finished as a piece of fine furniture.

"Yes, I like it very much indeed."

The carpenter beamed with pleasure to see that his work was appreciated.

"You can't do all this for five dollars, though," Cap said.

"That the price I gave you, sir. I don' expect no more."

"No, I want to be fair. And when you told me five, I'm sure you weren't counting on having to hire extra from the harness-maker and a blacksmith too. Do you think twenty dollars would be fair?"

"Five is all I ask."

"But you would be amenable to renegotiation, I assume."

"If you insist, sir, I won' gainsay you."

"Twenty it is then, and I thank you." Cap handed over a coin and laid the hickory gadget across his lap.

"I still think that is the ugliest thing I ever seen," Brown grumbled.

"Maybe so," Cap said without rancor. "The question, though, is whether it will do the job."

"Yes, suh. When we gonna find that out?"

"We'll stop by the gunsmith's and pick up my revolver. Then I want you to wheel me down by the river. Can you find a nice quiet place where no one else can see?"

"Yes, suh. They a place I know where the fish bite good. They's trees and bushes all over. Can't nobody see you there 'less they right up close beside."

"That sounds fine," Cap told him. He turned back to the carpenter and offered his hand. "Thank you, Mr. Moses. You've done nice work here."

"Yes, sir. Anytime, sir. You come again, hear?"

Cap shook the man's hand, then motioned for Brown to wheel him away.

Chapter Thirty-eight

The spot Cleofus Brown took him to was ideal. Close to town, but isolated by a screen of drooping trees and thick undergrowth. A bare, beaten stretch of earth beneath the leafy branches showed that the place was popular. Brown said he came here to fish. Cap guessed the spot might well be popular for other reasons too among those who had no privacy to count on. Certainly he could read sign easily enough to know that something more than fishing went on here. Wrestling matches, perhaps. He said nothing about that to Brown, however, for fear the man would think Cap was condemning the people who enjoyed the use of the riverbank here.

From Cap's point of view, the thing he liked best was the fact that the ground, in addition to being bare of fallen leaves, was hard-packed and should be easy to walk on.

Or whatever approximation of that simple act he could manage.

"Do you think you can get me into this rig?" he asked Brown.

"I can hold you up just fine, cap'n. We see 'bout the rest of it."

"Uh-huh." Cap frowned. And he felt the large-bore Remington revolver that was tucked away on the seat of the wheelchair beside his right leg.

One or the other of his new acquisitions would be proven useful today. He had determined that much during the weeks he'd lain helpless on a bed in Margaret's house.

Either he would find a way to get his mobility back, or he would by damn put a bullet through his own brain and keep himself from becoming a permanent liability to those he loved.

"I expect I'm ready if you are, Mr. Brown."

"Yes, suh. Just as you say."

Chapter Thirty-nine

The expensive and highly educated doctors in Omaha had told him the exact same thing the Virginia City barber had. A bullet fired from behind had shattered his hip, and he would never be able to walk again, primarily because the joint would never again be able to bear weight. The leg could be moved—thank goodness, else he would not be able to bend enough to sit—but the joint itself was useless.

With that in mind, Cap had given considerable thought to the construction of his device, and had taken great pains to make sure the carpenter who built it understood exactly what was wanted and why.

The wood-and-leather contraption consisted essentially of a harness rig that would strap tight around Cap's torso at chest and waist levels. It was this that was to carry the weight of his body, placing the burden above the shattered hip joint.

Below the tightly strapped torso rigging was a

wooden shaft something like the bottom half of an ordinary crutch, although in this instance it was affixed fairly solidly to Cap's torso rather than being held under an arm. The advantage, of course, was that he did not have to carry or manipulate anything with his hands.

If, that is, the rig worked at all.

And that remained to be seen.

"Are you ready, Mr. Brown?"

"Yes, suh."

"Lift me up then, if you please."

The powerful black man scooped Cap into his arms and held him more or less upright while Cap himself tugged the padded chest and waist straps snug and buckled them on as firmly as he could pull them.

Several abortive attempts to lean down to buckle the "leg" lightly to his own left leg proved impossible to manage on his own, however. He could bend easily enough, but once he did so, the wooden extension was swept behind his body, and he did not have either the strength or the dexterity to align his real leg with the artificial one.

"Maybe if I do up the leg straps first," he grumbled aloud.

"I don' think so, cap'n, suh. Whyn't you balance on your right leg while I strap up the left?"

"All right, we'll try that."

With Clee Brown providing a steadying hand to keep Cap from losing his balance while the fitting was completed, they got everything aligned, tugged, buckled, and in place.

"You sure looks unsteady," Brown said.

"Look, hell. You should try the way it feels." Cap whistled softly, then grinned.

"Careful now."

"No, don't grab me. I have to learn how to do this myself."

"Yes, suh." The words were in agreement, but the big man did not move away, and his hands were poised, ready to catch Cap should he lose his balance and topple over.

"Give me room, now. Give me room."

"Yes, suh." Brown did not move six inches from where he had been.

Cap swallowed and wiggled a little in a fruitless attempt to get a feel for the balance of the thing.

Then he took his first step.

Chapter Forty

"You all right, cap'n, suh?"

"Hell no, I'm not all right," Cap snapped back at the black man, who was bending over him, concern written over his dark features.

"You bleedin' anywhere, cap'n?"

"I don't think so," Cap responded without the least idea of whether he was or wasn't. "No, don't pick me up yet. Let me get my breath back first."

Cap looked himself over as best he could, but did not see any blood seeping through the cloth. Apparently his wounds were sufficiently well-healed, and they had not broken open when he'd fallen.

It felt, though, like his hip had been shattered all over again. Pain ripped and tore at his entire left side like a lance of pure fire, and if he hadn't been so stubborn, he would have burst into tears from it. As it was, it was all he could do to bear the agony without screaming.

He moved just a little and a fresh jolt of pain shot through him.

"You look pretty awful, cap'n. Pale. You know?"

He didn't know, but he could certainly believe it. "I should've thought to bring some of that laudanum the doctor gave me."

"I got me a pint o' cheap whiskey," Brown offered. "Not fit for a white man, like, but it's all we got."

Cap laughed. It was abrupt, and not exactly filled with joy, but it was a laugh nonetheless. "Mr. Brown, I've drunk Injun whiskey at rendezvous. There's nothing on earth you an' your friends could come up with to compare with that, I promise you."

Brown took a small pewter flask from somewhere inside the bib of his overalls and uncorked it before handing it to Cap, then he supported the old man's head so Cap could manage a drink.

The whiskey was raw on the tongue, but warm in the belly. Its heat spread quickly through him, taking at least some of the edge off the pain.

"Whew! Smooth," Cap said with a grin. He handed the flask back to Brown, who wiped the neck with his palm and then helped himself to a tot.

"Another, suh?"

"One more time," Cap agreed. He accepted the flask from Brown and drank. The second tasted considerably better than the first had.

"Cap'n, suh."

"Mmm?"

"You didn't wipe the neck of the bottle, suh."

Cap gave him a puzzled look.

"Cap'n, suh, I never seen no white man willing to drink after a nigger at all, much less do it without wipin' it down first."

"You're mighty easy impressed, Mr. Brown."

"You want another, suh?"

"No, thanks. Don't want to get so drunk I can't walk, y'know."

Brown chuckled and seated the cork back into the flask with a slap of his palm, then quickly made the flask disappear inside his overalls once more.

"Can you get me up again, Mr. Brown? I don't think I've quite got the hang of this just yet."

"You can call me Clee, cap'n."

"Why, thank you, Clee. I take that as a compliment."

"Yes, suh. That's just how it be meant, too." Brown smiled and very gently eased the old man back onto his two feet, the one natural one and the other not quite so.

Chapter Forty-one

"I think I've had about as much fun as I can enjoy for one day, Clee," Cap said. Fun. You bet. He felt about as battered and sore as he had after he was shot. He had fallen . . . he couldn't begin to count the number of times. He would try a step, lose his balance, fall down. Clee would pick him up again.

"I sure wisht you'd let me give you a little help, cap'n," Clee complained in a monotonous repeat of a litany he'd started a good half hour earlier.

"No, this is something I have to learn on my own," Cap insisted. As he had time and time again.

"Yes, suh. Whatever you say, suh."

"Clee, you could at least pretend to mean that sort of thing when you say it," Cap told him with a grin.

The big man laughed loudly and shook his head. "You not so easy to fool." He paused and added, "For a white man."

Cap let that one slide. "Help me out of this contraption and back into the chair, will you, please?

There's something else we have to do today."

"What's that, cap'n?"

"This gun. I'm going to get the hang of walking eventually. And that means I'll be needing the gun." Cap picked it up and examined it. "Fool thing. Never had much use for a short gun before. But if a man isn't willing to learn whatever is useful to him, then he'd be better off dead anyway."

"You be wanting that ammunition, then?"

Cap nodded. He had paid for the case of .44 rimfire cartridges earlier, but had told the gunsmith he would return to collect the small wooden crate later. At the time, he hadn't been so sure about that. Now he was. "We'll want a place to keep the cartridges, Clee. I don't want to show up at my daughter's home with those in my lap. Any ideas?"

"I can take care o' that, cap'n."

"Good. You can break the case and bring me, say, a couple boxes of cartridges every time we go out to practice. And when the case begins to run low, tell me about it. We'll order more."

"You real serious about learning to shoot that thing, cap'n," Brown observed.

"Dead serious," Cap said.

He meant it quite literally.

Chapter Forty-two

"You pure hell for accurate, cap'n. I give you that much."

"I've been at this, what? A week and a half now? I expect a man ought to be able to learn how a gun shoots in all that time. That's the whole idea of practicing with it."

"If'n you let me finish what I was tryin' to say here, cap'n . . . You mighty accurate with that short gun now. But you awful slow. Just real powerful slow, you are."

"What does slow have to do with anything?" Cap demanded.

"You ever seen one o' them gunfighters, cap'n?"

"Nope. Heard about them. Never saw such a thing."

"I did," Clee said. "Down in the Ozark country onct. Fella wanted another fella dead so he could have the other man's wife. O' course he made out it was for another reason, but them as knew what went on inside the walls o' the houses knew the

159

Frank Roderus

truth. Anyway, this fella wasn't much of a man. Real pretty fella, but what he had hangin' between his legs was for show. He didn't have no courage. So he up an' hired another fella to come all the way from Texas an' pick a fight. The one he hired was one of them gunfighter fellas." Brown snorted. "Fair fight they called it, but it wasn't no part of being fair. The gunfighter fella, he had time to roll a cigarette an' smoke it if he'd wanted to before the married man could get his pistol outta his pocket. That fella from Texas, he was almighty slick. Snatched his gun outta its pouch an' had the other fella dead before either one o' them had time to blink, cap'n. You think about that, hear?"

"And why should I care about that story of yours, Clee?"

"Cap'n, I may be one poor brute nigger, but I ain't as stupid as some seems to think. I know what you up to here. I heard 'bout your grandbaby an' I heard what happened to you after. Those men, they done wrong to your family an' they shot you full o' holes to boot. Now you expect to go after 'em. That's why you trying so hard to walk again, an' why you spend whole days burnin' powder an' usin' up lead. You gonna go out an' hunt for those same men again."

Cap did not bother trying to deny the obvious. "The law won't ever find them. I will."

"Yes, cap'n, I expect you will if'n you live long enough."

Cap grimaced. "There's no way I would consent to die, Clee, not until all three of those men are cold and in the ground."

"They shot you down onct, cap'n. What make you think they won't do it again?"

Cap gave Clee a hard and uncompromising look. "They just might do it again. They may even kill me this next time. But they won't get a chance to get behind me a second time, and I won't lay down and die until I've taken all three of them with me, so help me God."

"I don' know if He be interested in helpin' you do a thing like that, cap'n, but . . . can I speak free, cap'n?"

"Of course you can."

"Mista George, he pay me to take keer o' you. You know that much. He also pay me somethin' extra to tell on you, make sure you don' get in no trouble."

"Like going after those men?"

"Well, yes suh. I'm supposed to tell him if you plannin' anything. Mista George, he worried what his wife would think if he let her papa run off an' get himself killed, what with her already losing her baby an' then thinking she was gonna lose you too. Mista George thinks that would be too much for his wife. That's why he pays me to spy on you."

"He knows about the gun, then? All the practicing I've been doing?"

"Yes suh, cap'n. I been telling him every night after I take you in t'bed. I been spyin' on you. I'm sorry. Maybe I shouldn't a done that, but . . ."

"It's all right, Clee. I don't blame you. You're doing the job you were hired to do. After all, George is your employer really, not me."

"You ain't mad at me, cap'n?"

"No, Clee, I'm not mad at you. But when the time comes, I'll have to find a way to keep you from knowing what I'm up to so you won't be able to tell George about it."

"Cap'n, suh?"

"Yes, Clee?"

"I . . . I been thinkin' about that, see. An' well, if you don't mind me saying so, I don' think you would get along so good without me. I mean, you can't get into or out o' your walkin' harness without me helpin' you into it. You can't set down to the table or, excuse me, cap'n, you can't bend enough to take a dump without me to help you with the straps and stuff."

Cap scowled. "I know. I've been trying to think of a way around all that."

"I been thinking 'bout it too, cap'n. I know a way around it."

"You do?"

"Whyn't you hire me, cap'n? You don't have t'pay me much. I know you been spendin' heavy to buy the things you need an' gotta spend more to travel after those men. But if you hire me—just for my eats, that's all I need—if I'm workin' for you an' not for Mista George, then I can go along with you. Help you with what you need. An', well, an' then I wouldn't go about spying any more, 'cause it wouldn't be him I was working for, see, but you. Would you be willin' to do that, cap'n? I mean, I wouldn't ask you for eating money neither really, except I don't have money put back to carry me. Would that be all right, cap'n?"

"Lord, I reckon it would be more than all right, Clee. And don't you worry about your wages. I have some money put away down home in Santa Fe. I'll have a bank here—not the one George deals with, I think—I'll have a bank here wire home for the money we'll need." Cap smiled. "I won't let you go hungry, my friend. And I thank you for your kindness . . . and for your friendship. I didn't expect that of you."

"Yes, well, I didn't much expect it my own self, cap'n, if the truth be known."

Cap reached out and shook the big man's hand. "You just changed jobs, Clee. Now welcome to the family." He grinned.

Chapter Forty-three

He supposed they were about as ready as they were going to get. The lesser of his wounds no longer leaked, and by now hurt very little. And the doctors told him the hip was about as good as it was ever likely to become. Any further delay would be simple procrastination, and Cap had never been much for putting off a task, whether due to difficulty or pain. He did not intend to start backing down at this late stage of the game.

"I'm ready if you are, Clee."

"Yes, suh."

"You brought your things with you?"

Clee nodded. "I set my sack down under the bushes out back of the house, cap'n. Not that there's much. Just a change o' clothes an' my Bible."

"You're a God-fearing man, Clee?"

"Yes, suh. And I can read good too."

"Comes the time, Clee, you can read over the men I'm set to kill. Or me. Whatever."

"We'll talk about that some other time, all right?"

Frank Roderus

Cap nodded. "Dump my things into the carpetbag there, please, and drop it out the window. There's no sense arousing any worries in Margaret on our way out. I told her at breakfast I'd be going to the barber shop this morning."

"Yes, suh."

Clee made quick work of packing clothing and a few other things for the old man and lowering the bag to the ground outside Cap's bedroom window. The Remington revolver Cap customarily carried was tucked beside his leg beneath a lap robe. His spare leg, as he'd come to call it, rode strapped onto the back of the wheelchair.

Cap would have preferred to do without the nuisance of the chair, but both his mobility and his stamina were severely limited by the spare leg. He was able to walk without falling after long weeks of practice—and countless bruising falls—but the awkward hitch-and-swing gait necessitated by the contraption quickly sapped his strength. Too quickly for him to count on being able to walk very far at a time.

With the chair and Clee to push it, however, he felt sure he could do what had to be done. He only needed to be mobile without assistance when he actually found Rebecca's murderers. Until then he saw no reason why he shouldn't make use of Clee Brown and the chair to make that final moment possible.

Cap inspected the small platform Clee's carpenter friend had added at the back of the chair. Their baggage could ride there.

"You have your cartridges, cap'n?" Clee asked.

"A full cylinder in the gun and a pocketful to spare. I won't need more than that."

The black man nodded. "Got your money?"

"In the belt under my britches."

"Laudanum?"

"In the bag."

"Whiskey?"

"I thought you'd have that."

Clee chuckled. "I do, cap'n, suh. You know I do."

"I think we're ready. You, uh, didn't . . ."

"Not a word, suh. Not to Mista George nor nobody else."

"I've written out a note for Margaret. We can swing past the post office on our way to the wharf. I don't want to leave it for her, lest she find it too soon and do something to stop us from going."

"I expect you thought about 'most everything, cap'n."

"No, Clee, I'm sure that I haven't. But we'll just have to face whatever comes and deal with it one thing at a time." He reached inside his coat and checked for probably the tenth time that morning that he had the pair of steamer tickets he'd purchased the day before. The *Mandan Maid* was scheduled to depart Omaha at 1:15. They had plenty of time to board and find the stateroom Cap had booked for the westward passage.

"Mr. Brown," Cap said with a rising sense of eager anticipation, "let's you and me go see if we can't find some trouble to get into."

"I'll be right behind you, cap'n." Brown laughed. "And I surely do mean that most sincerely." With that he grasped the handles at the back of Cap's wheelchair and began to push the old man toward whatever fate had in store.

Chapter Forty-four

Going back up the Missouri was considerably more comfortable than his last trip downriver, Cap found. Not necessarily convenient, but comfortable enough.

Shallow-draft side-wheel river steamers were not, he also found, designed with wheeled chairs in mind.

He had booked a stateroom. But the chair would not fit through the narrow door opening.

He paid for meals on board. But freight was stacked so densely on the decks that the chair would not fit through the slender passageways left for use by the few passengers booked for the late-season trip.

If it had not been for Cleofus Brown, Cap was not sure he could have made the trip at all. As it was, Clee found ways to compensate for all the other problems.

The big man picked Cap up and carried him wherever he needed to go. He parked the chair more or less permanently on a small, clear patch of foredeck from which Cap could watch the boat's progress and enjoy the fall colors of the foliage drifting by. He took Cap to the dining table or, if the whim prevailed, brought food to the cabin for him.

The spare leg was left propped in a back corner of their cabin. Caulked tip or no, the rig proved simply too unstable for use on a sometimes slippery boat deck, and it would have been immeasurably awkward had Cap tried to walk through the tiny passages anyway.

As far as all that went, Cap was satisfied. But the weather bothered him. He worried about the winter that would soon set in.

The Missouri was low at this time of year, making the *Mandan Maid*'s progress even slower than normal, and Cap resented every hour of delay.

He had wasted most of the summer lying useless in a sickbed in Omaha, and now he worried that snow would block the overland routes away from Virginia City before he could so much as start his pursuit of the men who had murdered Rebecca.

"I still don't know why we goin' to this Virginia place anyhow," Clee told him at one point. "Those men you after, they'll be long gone from there, you know. Could be 'most anyplace after this long."

"I know that, Clee. But a cold trail is better than none. Besides, maybe we'll find someone there who knows something about them, or heard something, or just plain has a guess about where they went from Virginia City."

"Whatever you think, cap'n."

"I wish everybody had that same attitude," Cap said.

"You still worried about Miss Margaret, cap'n?"

"I am."

"You already done sent her letters from two landings 'long the way. She knows you all right, knows you got help with you." Clee grinned. "An' better for both of us that we travel too fast for her letters to catch up. You know? Can she find you with a letter, cap'n, she could come up the river herself an' catch you. You wouldn't want that, I reckon."

"No, I surely wouldn't want that," Cap agreed.

"Tell you what, cap'n. Tonight I'll fetch you more paper an' stuff. You write her another letter. Tell her somethin' make her feel good. Tell her you gonna take a quick look in this Virginia place an' then give up an' go home if'n you can't find out nothing new."

Cap thought over the suggestion and liked it. "I could tell her I intend to go on to San Francisco to see her sister. Margaret might accept that. She knows I haven't wanted to be a burden to her and George."

"See there, cap'n? You do that. Mail it from the next wood landing."

"I'll do that, Clee. Thanks."

"You want I should bring you something to eat now, cap'n? Something to drink?"

"I'm fine, Clee, thanks."

The big man nodded, but was not satisfied until he'd bent down and rearranged the robe that covered Cap's lap. Then he left Cap alone on the foredeck with his thoughts while Clee retired to a sun-warmed niche away from the biting north wind, where he could settle down and read his Bible, a pursuit that kept him occupied by the hour, without any indication of impatience.

Cap wished he could be as placid. Instead he found himself, as he did all too often on this trip, wishing he could pick the damned boat up and hurry it along. Early fall turned all too quickly to hard winter in this part of the country, and he did not want to be trapped in Virginia City until the spring breakup.

Chapter Forty-five

Clee Brown removed the lashings that tied the wheelchair and their baggage atop the freight load, then lifted it all down as easily as if the bulky chair consisted of nothing more than a few twigs of wicker. Cap found the big man's power to be thoroughly amazing. Once the chair was ready, Clee lifted Cap down from the wagon and placed him into the chair. Clee looked around and made a sour face.

"It isn't much to look at," Cap agreed, "but Virginia City is mean clear through. At least that's the impression I got the last time I was here."

"Where to now, cap'n?"

Cap pointed toward The Glory Hole, Barney Smith's saloon. Nothing had been done to change it in the past few months, which Cap was not sure if he should take as a good sign or a bad one. Business had not been so good that the place had needed to expand. But then it was still here, still conducting trade. That was not always a given in a mining camp, some of which were so short-lived they did not survive from one season into the next. The Glory Hole could at least lay claim to that amount of durability as the sharp scent of ozone on a cold wind gave proof enough that up here summer had already given way to fall . . . and winter was likely not very far behind.

"In here, cap'n?"

"Please."

Clee muscled the chair, luggage and all, onto the narrow boardwalk in front of the saloon and pushed inside. Young Smith was tending bar for a very few customers when he saw Cap and broke into a welcoming smile. He threw a towel onto the bar surface and hurried to meet his visitor.

"I never expected to see you here again, Captain. To tell you the truth, I didn't think you would make it down the river alive. I'm glad to be proved wrong."

Cap shook the young man's hand. "Can I have my room back for a night or two?"

"You can have anything I've got. You know that."

"You'll help me then, I take it?"

Smith frowned a little. "Help you, sir? In what way?"

"I need some information, Barney. From anyone who got to know those men when they were in town. I, uh . . . I assume they haven't come back here. Have they?"

"The ones who shot you? No, they wouldn't show their faces in this town again. Not after the boys here heard what they did to your granddaughter. They wouldn't any of them last five minutes here without finding themselves wearing a hemp necktie." Barney took a moment to look Clee over. When he spoke, it was not to Brown, but to Cap again. "Your man is big, sir, but he doesn't look like a gun-

171

man to me. And I never heard of a ni—uh, Negro lawman."

"Clee is my friend, Barney, and my transportation. He's along to help me, not to arrest anybody."

"I see," Barney said, sounding like he did not see what Cap meant at all. "I, uh . . . I can ask around. See if anybody knows anything he hasn't already told."

"I would appreciate it, son." Cap smiled and changed the subject. "If it's all right with you, then, we'll put our things in the room and go find a proper meal. It's been a long and not particularly pleasant trip to get here, and I could use some supper and a good night's sleep. Come morning, we'll see can we get a handle on where those murderers might've run to this time."

"Yes, sir. If you like."

Chapter Forty-six

"Sure, I remember those guys. Uh, look, could I have a drink? Barney said maybe you'd buy me a drink. I, uh, I ain't been making out too good. At my claim, I mean. It ain't all I thought it'd be. To tell you the truth, mister, if it don't start to show any better color than it's been lately, I won't try and hang on here through the winter. I'll sell off whatever I can and try again over in Idaho. That's where the next good pickings are gonna be. Everybody says so. I might just try my luck over there. About that drink, mister . . ."

Cap nodded, and Clee Brown went to fetch a short whiskey for the miner. It was somewhere in the neighborhood of eight o'clock in the morning, and Brown had only minutes earlier brought Cap back from breakfast at the cafe he'd never gotten to eat in the last time he'd visited Virginia City.

"What I'm wanting to know, Mr. Lucas, is about the men Barney said were your neighbors during the little while they stayed here. Art Coffrey, Everett

Shear, and Thomas Rayne. Do you remember them?"

Lucas swallowed off half the whiskey in a first, avid gulp, then seemed to relax a little as he leaned against the back of his chair and gave the old man a small smile. "Sure, I remember them. They're the ones shot you all to pieces, aren't they?"

Cap nodded.

"We all thought you was dead, mister. So did they, I expect. But they ran off anyhow. By then everybody'd heard what you said about them. Most o' the boys, I don't mind telling you, they didn't believe the things you said those men did. I kinda thought all along you was telling the truth. But then I seen more of them than just about anybody else did, see. I already figured they wasn't the kind of neighbors a man cozies up to." Lucas drank the rest of his whiskey and looked expectantly toward Clee, who waited for an affirming nod from Cap before going for a refill.

"You say you had doubts about them already?" Cap prodded.

"Sure. Then o' course everybody did once they run off. I expect if they'd stayed put and toughed it out they coulda convinced most that they hadn't never done stuff to your little girl." Lucas shook his head sadly. "Sure was a shame, that. Just a baby, I heard."

Cap did not bother elaborating either on Rebecca's age or on their relationship. "About the three men?"

"Yes, sure. Just a second." Lucas accepted the second whiskey and poured half of it on top of the first. "Like I was saying."

"Uh-huh."

"They moved in on the claim next to mine. Said they paid Donny Albright five hundred dollars hard money for it, but I knew right off that was a lie. Last I seen Donny, he'd already packed his gear, what little of it he hadn't sold, and was pulling out. Had a bindle on his shoulder and dust on his shoes. You know?"

Cap didn't, but he nodded anyway.

"Donny, he was a pretty honest old boy too. Good neighbor. Always willing to share his johnnycake, whatever he had. Couldn't cook worth a damn, but what he had he'd share. An' the thing is, see, bad as my claim is, Donny's was worse. Worse? Mister, it was useless. He'd found a little scratch dust when he first looked, else he wouldn't have filed his claim. I mean, the rules say you got to show some color in order to make a proper filing, but not everybody bothers. They just throw down some stakes and swear they found something to justify the claim. You know? Donny, he was so honest it hurt. I'd swear to God Almighty that Donny found at least that pinch of stray dust else he wouldn't have sworn that he did. Then he come to find out there wasn't more to be had. I dunno, maybe what he found was what some other fella went an' spilled outta his poke on his way home from a drunk night out. You know?"

"Sure, I know."

"Right. O' course you do. Say, could I have just one more o' these, maybe?"

Cap nodded. Clee fetched. Lucas drank.

Cap sighed. "You were saying, Mr. Lucas?"

"Right. About those fellas that shot you. They said they paid Donny five hundred for that bald-headed claim of his. But I knew Donny pretty good by then. He'd've told those men the truth about his claim, an' if they paid him anything for title to it . . . and I expect they must've because they had them a quitclaim deed with Donny's signature on

Frank Roderus

it. Which I'm sure of because I seen Donny sign stuff before. It was his mark, no mistake about it."

"Uh-huh," Cap repeated, wishing Lucas would come to the point.

"You see, if Donny asked money for his claim, it was more likely five dollars than five hundred. Which those fellas didn't look like they'd had to begin with, if you see what I mean."

"Yes, I do," Cap said.

"But the really funny thing about those fellas was the first day they worked that hole, they told how they'd got lucky an' toted up more than eighty dollars in flakes. Even funnier, the night before they made that money, or so they said, Leroy Bruner's place was robbed while he was at Sadie's place having his back problems straightened out. Somebody broke into Leroy's cabin and found his squirrel-hole under the hearth. Which is a dumb place t'hide your poke to start with, since half the idiots I know do the same dang thing. But anyhow, that's where Leroy kept his savings, and somebody took it off him that selfsame night. More than seven hundred worth to hear Leroy tell it, which prob'ly means it was anyway over a hundred dollars in those flat, pounded little flakes that he took outta the creekbed at his claim." Lucas grinned, exposing pale gums and a scattering of brown teeth. "Mind you, I ain't saying that those fellas are the ones that stole Leroy's poke. But I thought it mighty queer that Donny could've worked that claim three and a half months without taking enough to buy a jug of trade whiskey, then those fellas come in an' first thing sack up that kinda money."

"They wanted your friend Donny's useless claim, you think, so they would have an excuse to walk around with gold dust in their pokes?" Cap asked.

"That's exactly what I mean, mister. I surely do."

"And do you have any idea where they would have gone when they skeedaddled out of Virginia City after the shooting?"

Lucas shrugged. "I didn't see them go, mind, so I can't say nothing for sure. But they didn't head down toward the river. Your friend Barney looked into that for you. And I doubt they'd go south. They say that country straight south hasn't never yet been looked at by a single white man. There's no trails there for a man to follow, nothing like that at all."

Cap knew better, but again there was no point in trying to educate Lucas on the subject. Besides, it was very likely that the mistaken belief the Virginia City miner had about the supposedly inhospitable terrain to the south was very much the same that Shear, Rayne, and Coffrey would have had.

"They had horses, didn't they?"

"Yes, sir, they had horses when they come here an' horses when they left, so I'd say it's pretty certain they went off a-horseback. Moving fast and staying outta sight until they were clear of town, likely. Then," the man shrugged, "who knows?"

Cap thumbed his chin for a moment. "You say talk is that Idaho is the next place to strike and boom?"

"Ayuh, that's what everyone says. I've heard more than a few say they're thinking of heading Idaho way come spring."

"Would the mining men around here know about the Lolo Trail?" Cap asked.

"O' course. You don't think we're ignorant, do you? That's the trail runs over toward those Idaho diggings and on to the Oregon country, Walla Walla, all them places."

"So my men might well have gone across into Idaho," Cap mused out loud.

"Sure. But then they coulda went to Boston for all I or anybody else would know for sure, mister. I mean, I'm sorry as all hell about what happened to your little girl, an' I hope some town marshal fetches up with those fellas someday. But was I you, I wouldn't count on it a whole helluva lot. They're gone far from here, wherever they are, and you can't paper the whole dang country with wanted fliers, now can you?"

Cap's answering smile was grim and without any trace of mirth. "It wasn't paper that I had in mind for doing them in," he said.

Cap looked past the miner's shoulder to where Clee was keeping a watchful eye on things around them. "Bring the gentleman one more drink, please, Mr. Brown. Then we have some arrangements to make, if you would be so kind."

"Yes suh, cap'n. Just as you say."

Chapter Forty-seven

"With all due respect, cap'n, I think you may've gone and lost your mind. Sir."

"And may I ask what you suggest we do instead, Mr. Brown?"

"Something a whole lot more sensible than what you got in mind, cap'n. Like go back down to the railroad. I dunno, go back to the river an' take a boat and then go west again from Omaha like you and Mista George done before, or take that road the army keeps up, the one you told me those fellas came north on."

"And from there, Clee?"

"West. Far as the tracks run. You know Mista George could arrange that. Then . . . I dunno how far that would be. We'd find a way to this Idaho place from there. You could do that. I know you could."

Cap nodded. "Certainly we could take that route. Probably find a coach going into Deseret from end-of-track. Then maybe another one north from there. Of course by the time we got to Deseret it would be the dead of winter. Travel might not be so easy. Who knows, we might even have to wait until spring."

"You wouldn't wait that long nohow, cap'n."

"No, and I won't waste time going the long way around either. If there is any chance at all that those men might be somewhere in the Idaho diggings, my friend, I want to find them before spring. I don't think they are the sort to put down roots or make any lasting friendships wherever they go. I'd think by the time the trails open up next spring they'll be ready to move again. They might even split up, and that could make the situation impossible. If I can, I'd certainly rather locate them all at once and get this thing over with. I don't want any single one of them to get away from me, Clee. I hope you understand that."

"Yes suh, cap'n, I do. But I still think you oughta change your mind about what you fixing to do this time."

Cap chuckled. "I admit it isn't exactly an ordinary sort of plan, but I can't think of a better one. Unless you can come up with some suggestion for how me, my spare leg, and this chair can all fit in a saddle."

"No suh, cap'n. We both knows better than that. You won't never sit on top o' no horse again do you live to Methuselah's age an' then some. But I got t'say, suh, that you are plumb outta your mind, thinking what you're wantin' to do this time."

"Clee, it could be that this time you're right. We shall see. But in the meantime, it would please me if you would take me to see Mr. Magruder."

"Whatever you say, cap'n. Whatever you say, suh." The big man took hold of the handles on the back of Cap's chair and gave the conveyance a shove that was hard enough to express his doubts and displeasure.

Chapter Forty-eight

Philip Magruder turned out to be a large man with cheeks made red by constant exposure to the cut of cold winds. When Cap found him, he had his sleeves rolled up and was elbow-deep in a tub of evil-smelling oils, emollients, and for all Cap knew sorcerer's potions as well.

Cap's nose wrinkled in protest to the assault on his sensibilities. "What *is* that stuff, anyway?"

Magruder looked up from his labors with a happy grin. "Harness dressing. My own mix. Sure you want to know what's in it?"

Cap laughed and shook his head. "On second thought, friend, we're probably better off not knowing."

Magruder looked first at Cap, then at Clee. "And the two of you would be . . . ?"

Cap introduced himself, then said, "Mr. Brown here constitutes my legs. Hands and arms sometimes too." He lowered his voice to a stage whisper. "He's a blackamoor, you know."

"Do tell," Magruder said. "Are you sure about that?"

Cap shrugged. "Perhaps not. I haven't looked him all over to make sure of it, but I have my suspicions."

Magruder chuckled, then reached for a rag that he used to wipe his hands and lower arms free from most of the stinking concoction he was mixing. "Pleased to meet you." He offered a shake first to Cap and then to Clee. Cap liked that. Not everyone took to the idea of having a black man in close quarters for any extended period of time. Apparently Philip Magruder was not one of those.

"You would be the gent who was near killed by those three thieves a few months back, wouldn't you?" Magruder observed after a moment's thought on the subject.

"I would," Cap admitted.

"They're long gone from here, you know."

Cap nodded. "So we've been told."

Magruder gave Clee another looking over. "You weren't thinking of having them thrashed or anything like that, were you?"

"I was not. Mr. Brown provides me with mobility, not retribution."

"Uh-huh." Magruder went back to his tub of harness dressing, adding a sparkling powder of some sort from a box, then sniffing critically at the result for a moment before adding a dash more. He began to stir the mess, which, after the introduction of whatever the powder was, seemed to smell a little less objectionable, Cap thought. Either that or he was becoming used to the stink. "I don't know where they've gotten to if that's what you're here to ask after."

"No, Mr. Magruder. It's my understanding that

you're a specialist in hauling large objects by mule train."

Magruder looked up and beamed with pleasure. It was obvious that this was a man who thoroughly liked what he did and was comfortable in the knowledge that he was very good at it. "I am, sir. The best this side of . . ." he paused, frowned, then said, "Never mind this side of anywhere. I'm the best there is. My babies carried an entire steam-powered stamp mill up from Cherry Creek to Idaho Springs before the roads were cut through. Carried it all, boiler included, with naught but my babies."

"Idaho," Cap said. "You know Idaho, then?"

Magruder laughed. "Idaho Springs, Mr. Marsden, is in Colorado Territory. Has nothing to do with the country west of here. But since you ask, yes, I know a bit about Idaho too. I've hauled in and out of this camp pretty much since the discovery."

"And across the mountains into Idaho as well?"

"Oh, yes. Pierce, Orofino, all those. My babies and me have made that trip a dozen times or more."

"You could make it again now? Before winter closes the passes, do you think?"

"I would say so. Of course, nothing comes with guarantees when it comes to nature and the whims of God. But I think there's time enough. My mules aren't as bothered by a little snow as wagons would be."

"How did you haul that steam boiler, Mr. Magruder?"

His big man's grin became all the broader. "Simple when you know how, Mr. Marsden. I knocked it down into manageable pieces, each of them weighing not more than four, five hundred pounds. Then I rigged slings with one stout mule at either end and the load suspended between them. It took two trips, sixty mules each time, but I got it all

183

there, reassembled and operating without losing a single piece."

Cap grunted. "Not on a travois but suspended," he mused.

"That's right. Travois would be like to break with that much weight on it, and the skids would wear down in no time even if they didn't break. Be too much for one mule to pull, besides. A sling, that's the best way. Why, I could carry a ship's mast all in one piece if I didn't have tight turns to make. Just put enough of my babies to the task, and harness them in pairs with the load swung between. Yes, sir, there's not hardly a load that me and my babies can't carry."

"Now I'm real pleased to hear you say that, Mr. Magruder, because Mr. Brown and I have a commission for you. A load I want carried over to the Idaho discoveries quick while the passes are still usable."

Magruder gave his harness dressing a critical examination and then, satisfied, began using a dipper to decant the black, oily stuff into a succession of flasks, bottles, and canteens he'd laid ready to store and transport the liquid.

"Whatever it is, Mr. Marsden, I can haul it. If we can agree on a price, sir, I'll get your goods wherever you want them taken. You have my word on it."

"In that case, Mr. Magruder, I believe we can do some business together."

Chapter Forty-nine

Cap winced. A sling suspended hammocklike between two mules was not as comfortable as riding as a steamboat passenger. But then it was not nearly so painful as the jolting of a wagon would have been or, worse, the bang and thump of a travois being dragged over rough ground.

He could feel the somewhat muted jar of the mules' footfalls, but there was only real pain involved on those rare occasions when one of Mr. Magruder's "babies" stumbled.

Babies indeed, Cap thought with no small amount of amusement. Magruder had assembled a train of the biggest, heaviest-bodied Missouri mules Cap had ever seen in his life. And as a participant—well, sort of, if only in a secondhand sort of way—in the Santa Fe trade, Cap Marsden had seen many and many a mule over the past several decades.

Philip Magruder, it seemed, had an eye for excellence when it came to mules, and a consuming affection for the lanky, brown-eyed creatures that made the man willing to talk about them endlessly at the slightest opening or opportunity.

"All my babies are bred out of the finest draught mares. The really big breeds, I mean. No plain cobs for these babies, mind. Percheron, Belgian, and like that. Do you see that pair of blacks over there? Seventeen hands and one, the nearer of them is. His brother is seventeen two and a bit over. They're both bred out of a Shire mare. Do you know the breed, sir?"

Cap shook his head. "I haven't had the pleasure."

"Then you've missed something, sir, I tell you true." Magruder laughed. "I found the dam on a farm in Iowa. First time I ever saw a Shire too. They aren't common. Kind of an odd man, the farmer with the Shire. Talks like a German though his family is said to've been in this country for half a dozen generations back. From someplace in Pennsylvania, I think. Dresses funny too. All in black. And no buttons on his vest. Told me buttons are sinful. Damned if I could figure out why, though he tried more than once to explain. I still wish I understood it. It bothers me, wondering about that, but between us we didn't have the words to make it clear. Anyway, this man, he had just about the prettiest mare I ever did see. He took me out to his barn—an awful lot finer building than his house, it was—and the first stall I looked into I saw this immense, fine horse, black with white lower legs and a white snip. Handsome. I was impressed and asked if the horse pulled as good as it looked. This farmer, he gave me an odd look and said it was too soon to know, that the animal wasn't but a yearling. And it so big I couldn't reach its poll when it lifted its head. Already had feet on it like serving platters. Never mind plate-sized hoofs. This yearling had feet like platters.

"I knew right then and there I had to have me some mules out of that mare. Told the man so. He said he couldn't possibly waste a year's breeding of that prize mare to produce a mule. Seems this man was a horse fancier. Didn't know any better, I suppose. Didn't understand mules. He said he wasn't interested in breeding them."

Magruder chuckled. "He kept telling me that right up until I told him how much I'd pay for a year's use of his mare. That changed his mind. So as soon as the mare was old enough to be bred, I leased a big jack I knew of down in Missouri and took it north. I stood the jack with him and while I had it under contract let it out for stud services in the area with this farmer—he was an honest man if a little strange in some ways, I'll say that for him— with him acting as my manager to put the jack to other mares while it was there. The arrangement lasted two years and I got these two fine babies out of the mare, but then she took sick and couldn't carry a foal to term again afterward. The mare still looks all right, but she can't breed anymore. Like to broke my heart, that did. His too, I think, because he never got the Shire stud he wanted out of her and now never will. But I got these two boys out of her, and do I ever find another Shire, or hear of where I can buy one, I'll breed more like them. They're the best. But then all my babies are. I won't bother feeding an animal that isn't top-notch. When it comes to my babies, the best there is is the least I'll put up with."

And Magruder did know his trade. Cap had to give him that.

For the trip into Idaho, Magruder had put together a short train of exceptionally fine mules.

Two pairs were rigged with slings, one to carry Cap in his hammock and the other to carry the bulky wheeled chair.

Clee Brown was mounted astride—on a mule, of course, not a horse, which Cap doubted Magruder would have allowed near his string of pampered babies—and their few pieces of luggage were transported on ordinary packframes carried by single mules.

In addition to Cap and his equipage, Magruder had found enough other freight to justify bringing another half dozen mules and one helper to assist with the twice-daily loading and unloading.

Magruder insisted that his mules be completely unloaded at midday so they could eat and rest comfortably.

And, Cap noted, the helper, a dim-witted fellow named Jack with more salt than pepper in his beard and breath worse than that of the mules, was never asked to feed or groom the mules, just perform the manual labor of loading or unloading them.

Magruder trusted only himself to dole out each mule's portion of mixed grain, to assure himself that each hoof in the string was clean and free from lodged pebbles, to brush and curry each animal's back each and every time the animal was unloaded.

Cap doubted he had ever seen a human baby taken half such good care of as Philip Magruder's babies.

There was no question, though, that the man knew his business. He was a thoroughgoing professional, and Cap was pleased with his choice of freighter to get them across the mountains to the Idaho diggings where Everett Shear, Thomas Rayne and Art Coffrey might—please God let them be there, Cap silently begged a dozen times or more each day—be found.

Chapter Fifty

He hated to admit it even to himself—and would not have admitted it aloud to any soul then living— but Old Marsden was lost.

The man who'd found his way through the Shining Mountains year after year had no idea where he was now or where he ought to be.

Pierce, they'd said. Orofino. Gold strikes on the tributaries of the Snake. Well, Cap knew the Snake. Of course he did. There was scarcely a river west of Kentucky or cast of California—he made an exception about California because after all, what mountain man in his right senses cared about it anyway?—that Cap Marsden did not know.

As for places called Pierce and Orofino, well, when Cap roamed this country from beaver dam to rendezvous and back again, there weren't any places. Not the sort that had names anyway, except those few names the boys of the trapping brigades chose to give them. This hole or that creek or some other peak or camp or reminder.

But the Snake, of course he knew the Snake. Hudson's Bay Company had them a trading post far up the Snake. Fort Hall, it was. Cap had been there three different times, twice because he wanted to go and once when some officious popinjays who thought they were the queen's right-hand boys made a false arrest.

So naturally he'd thought when they said the Snake they meant Fort Hall and that neighborhood.

That wasn't at all where Philip Magruder was taking him now.

And the ragged, jumbled maze of rock, creeks, and barren forest they were traversing now was nothing Cap knew from the past. Nor, for that matter, was it country that he especially wanted to come to know.

Big as the country was, it was almost lifeless. Even the deer and elk and moose seemed uninterested in it, and if a man didn't carry food along with him, he would starve somewhere between walk-in and crawl-out.

Beaver? Not a one, nor any sign of abandoned or decaying old dams. There were water and creeks, but none of the young, tasty—if you were a beaver, that is—saplings that constituted most of the beaver's food and building materials.

There weren't beaver now and there hadn't been in a very long time, if ever.

It was no wonder, Cap conceded, that he and his companions hadn't found reason to trap their way through here before. No wonder he did not know this particular stretch of country.

Magruder, on the other hand, was entirely comfortable here. He displayed no doubts or hesitation about the route he needed to take to reach the Idaho gold diggings. The man went along, cheerful as a sunrise and mindful of his mules, with no notion whatsoever that his client was ignorant of this patch of mountains.

Cap thought the sensible thing was to let matters continue just exactly that way, so he kept his mouth shut and his eyes open and tried to figure out just where it was they were off to along a path a good ninety degrees off what would have taken them down to the Fort Hall country that he did know and remembered.

Chapter Fifty-one

Cap wrapped his hands loosely around the enameled metal cup. Loosely because the coffee was piping hot. But close because his aching joints yearned for the warmth. The air was biting cold. He looked over to the big freighter and asked, "How much longer, Mr. Magruder?"

Magruder shrugged. "Four days, five maybe."

Cap grunted and closed his eyes. He tipped his head back and breathed in through his nose, taking the air deep and holding it there. Then he opened his eyes again and frowned.

"Mr. Magruder."

"Aye?"

"We're in trouble."

"How do you figure that, Mr. Marsden?"

"There's snow coming."

Magruder stood and peered out across the waves of mountain peaks that stretched endlessly to the north. The midday sky there was clear, a crystalline blue unblemished by any taint of cloud or haze.

Magruder pondered the sight for several long moments, then turned back to face the old man in the wheelchair and said, "I don't think so, Mr. Marsden."

Cap took a swallow of his coffee and tightened his grip on the cup. Already the coffee was starting to cool, and he could now hold tight to the metal without discomfort. "It's coming, Mr. Magruder. I can smell it on the air."

"You aren't familiar with this country, sir," Magruder disagreed. "Believe me, you don't have anything to worry about."

"I hope you're right," Cap told him. "Clee."

"Yes, suh?"

"There's something I'd like you to do when we make camp this evening. I want you to take one of the spare blankets. A good one, mind. Don't go looking for one with holes in it or one that's worn thin in spots. Take one of the new ones we bought for the trip and cut it into eight pieces. You have a good knife?"

"I do, suh."

"Good."

"Eight pieces?"

"That's right. And we'll need eight thongs or lengths of twine. Almost anything will do for that, though, just so it's fairly stout. Doesn't have to take much strain."

"Mind if I ask what I'm makin' with all that, cap'n?"

"Mittens, Mr. Brown. We're going to need four pairs of heavy mittens. We'll need foot wraps too, but if it comes to that we can mound ground litter, old needles or leaves or whatever, for that. Just pile it knee-deep and everybody huddle close together. Comes the time, we'll look for a windbreak if we can find one, or build one if necessary. We'll be all right, though. I've sat through worse than this is gonna be."

Clee too stared out to the north where the winter storms should originate. "Mr. Magruder says there won't be no storm, cap'n."

Old Marsden looked at the black man and smiled. "So he did, Mr. Brown. So he did."

"You want more o' that coffee, cap'n?"

"Yes, I would, Clee. Thank you." Cap held his cup out for Brown to freshen, then turned his coat collar high. Never mind what the young and vigorous and undoubtedly experienced freight master claimed. The snow was coming. Cap could smell it.

Chapter Fifty-two

It started as a thin, faint line of gray limning the horizon far to the west. It became visible late in the forenoon of the following day and raced swiftly eastward, looming taller and taller until it dominated the skyline in a mass of charcoal-gray cloud.

"There's a canyon about two miles on, Mr. Marsden," Magruder told him. "We'll make a run for that and lay out a camp. From the looks of this, we may be here a spell."

Cap shook his head. "I don't think that would be wise."

"We have to take shelter," Magruder insisted. "We can't move through weather like that looks to be. We'll have to wait until it stops blowing. Then we can pick up and move on again."

"Oh, I agree we have to sit it out," Cap said. "But not in your canyon."

"But that's the logical—"

"No, sir. It isn't. If you take us down low, Mr. Magruder, we're apt to be snowbound there. I've seen blows like this before. You can't believe the amount of snow this storm will carry. Enough to fill a gulch or small canyon if the wind direction is right. We can't risk being at the bottom of a thirty-foot drift, sir. We could be buried alive." Cap softened his warning with a smile. "I don't know about you, Mr. Magruder, but that isn't in my plan for things."

"Everybody knows you have to take shelter from a bad storm, Mr. Marsden. What is it you suggest, if not looking for a place to camp?"

"Oh, we have to shelter, all right. But not down there. We'll shelter high. On the windward face of a slope and close to the top. That way the snow will blow over us and collect on the other side of the ridge."

"If we stay in the wind we'll freeze to death. How's it better to freeze than be buried?"

"With a windbreak, Mr. Magruder. We'll hole up in a cave if we find one or under an overhang. If there isn't anything natural to help, we'll make for ourselves. Chop saplings and small trees to make a lean-to and thatch it with pine boughs. Lord knows there's enough material around to build with. And we have time. It'll be some hours before it gets here. With three sets of hands to do the work—I'd pitch in if I could—there's time enough. If we can find a deadfall or a blowdown, so much the better. It would give us wood to keep a fire going. The windbreak will reflect heat as well as block the worst cut of the wind. We won't have to be under cover to make it through comfortably enough, and we won't risk being trapped at the bottom of some cut or canyon."

"I don't know, Mr. Marsden, I—"

"But I do know, Mr. Magruder. Believe me. I know what I'm talking about. I spent years in the

Shining Mountains back when there wasn't anything out here but wild Injuns and fat beaver. Believe me. Please."

Magruder looked skeptical.

"The cap'n don't look like much no more, Mista Magruder suh, but he smart an' he nervy. I'm gonna stay an' do whatever he say," Clee Brown put in. "Me and him, we stay where he say even if you an' Jack wanta go on without us."

"And leave some of my babies behind?" Magruder sounded like that thought was purely scandalous.

Clee shrugged. "Take 'em with you if you want. They yours. We still stay where the cap'n say."

"I can't ride away and leave a client to die," Magruder snapped.

"Just do what the cap'n say, suh. He knows what he talkin' about."

"It doesn't sound right to me. Not at all right. What would I do with my babies if we make a windbreak for ourselves?"

"Put them on a picket rope where they can put their butts to the wind," Cap said. "They should be all right."

"What if the storm lasts for days?"

"Oh, it will. I can almost promise you that it will. But we'll all make it through, including your mules. They won't be able to forage for food, but there will be more than enough snow for them to eat. They'll manage."

"I still say it doesn't sound right to me," Magruder insisted.

Cap looked at Brown. "You would stay with me if Mr. Magruder feels he should go ahead without us?"

"Yes, suh. I expect I would."

Cap nodded. "That's our decision, Mr. Magruder.

You're welcome to make your own in regard to your animals and your man."

Magruder grumbled and muttered. But he stood in his stirrups to peer out to the west. After a moment he settled back onto his saddle and said, "There's a blowdown about a half mile off the regular trail. I've seen it from a distance before. It isn't far from here."

"It's on a west-facing slope?" Cap asked.

"Aye, it is."

"Then I suggest, sir, that you take us there with all possible haste. We'll want as much time as we can get to prepare."

Frowning and still reluctant, Magruder nudged his saddle mule to the head of the long, thin train, and led the way directly toward the approaching storm.

Chapter Fifty-three

The men, those who were physically able, worked with the impetus of fear to drive them. Safety was days away, save for whatever of it they could make for themselves. And survival is a powerful motivation.

Cap lay on a bed of pine boughs cut and prepared for him by Clee Brown. Among the packs of freight being carried on the mules, Magruder had a bale of trade blankets destined for sale in the Idaho gold camps along with other consignments of rock hammers, gold pans, and quicksilver. Magruder broke open the blankets and distributed them so each man had five blankets to huddle beneath.

Even that, Cap suspected, might not be enough to maintain body warmth if the storm lasted for an extended length of time. If it did, however, the four could bunch together, piling their entire supply of blankets over them and sharing what warmth they had along with the misery they would also undoubtedly share in equal portions.

Frank Roderus

Throughout the early afternoon, Magruder, Jack, and Clee scurried to erect a lean-to to act as both windbreak and heat reflector. At Cap's direction, they placed the lean-to five feet or so from the rock face of a sloping hillside overlooking the blowdown Magruder had led them to. The long dead trees would provide a virtually inexhaustible supply of firewood. Unless, that is, the blowdown disappeared beneath a burden of snow.

As soon as the lean-to was complete, fashioned from living trees, the men turned their attention to the collection of firewood from the age-dried blowdown.

Most of the wood lay in a depression at the foot of the slope and would be vulnerable to the drifts that were sure to build as the storm emptied itself. Cap made sure the men gathered wood from down low now while they still could, leaving the nearer trees, those that had fallen higher on the hillside, for collection later when the gathering might not be so easy.

With Clee Brown and Jack gathering limbs, branches, and whole trees small enough to be dragged up the slope, Magruder used a collapsible bow saw to cut the wood ready for stacking at either end of the lean-to, where it would be readily accessible no matter the weather.

Cap approved of Magruder's choice of the saw for the purpose. Sensible. Cold, long-dead timber and axes in chilled fingers are a sure recipe for disaster. And no one ever accidentally lost a foot or set of toes to a Swedish bow saw.

Magruder's "babies" were tied to a picket line strung a rod and a half downslope from the lean-to where the men would shelter. They were placed facing up the hillside so their backsides would be presented to the wind, their eyes and muzzles as protected as it would be possible to make them. There was no forage available for them. The mules would have to survive without food until the storm ended, as there were not even cottonwoods or other trees nearby with bark that could be stripped and eaten by the livestock.

By the time night fell and the men had to stop working for lack of ability to see their footing on the graveled hillside, they had virtual mountains of downed wood thrown up at both ends of the lean-to, and all their supplies had been transferred inside the pocket of warmth created by the fire which Cap kept blazing while the others worked out in the cold wind.

Magruder stepped inside and stripped off his gloves to hold his hands out to the fire. He craned his neck and peered up through the roofless gap between the top of the lean-to and the nearly vertical rock wall Cap had chosen for their refuge. There were no stars visible. High clouds, dark even before the coming of night, obscured the sky from one horizon to the next. A rising wind began to moan and keen through the boughs of the young pines that had survived the old blowdown. But there was as yet no hint of snow in the swirling air.

"I'm thinking we might've wasted a lot of time an' work alike," Magruder said. "Could be this is all smoke and no fire, if you know what I mean."

"No snow, you mean," Cap said.

"Aye. You'd think it would've started by now if it was going to. The front of those clouds passed over two, three hours back."

"If I'm wrong, Mr. Magruder, I will apologize come tomorrow. Profusely. And with pleasure."

"But you still don't think so, is that it?" Magruder asked.

"Ask me again at dawn tomorrow."

Magruder grunted noncommittally and accepted the steaming cup of coffee Clee Brown handed to him. Clee served Cap, Magruder, and Jack, then opened his coat wide to the heat of the fire and hunkered close beside it with his own tin cup.

Chapter Fifty-four

They woke to a world that was opaque and nearly devoid of color. The only forms that had substance or hue were those within the very close confines of their own tiny shelter. Everything else around them might have disappeared off the face of the earth for all they could see of it.

Occasional snowflakes, huge and unusually wet, escaped the howling press of the wind that lashed at the western face of the lean-to and leaped on up the slope above it. Those few flakes danced in tiny eddies that were clearly visible in the density of the storm, danced and then drifted softly down onto the men while the great mass they escaped from swept harmlessly overhead.

"I still think it's going to snow," Cap said with a grin as Magruder stomped unhappily back from the side of their shelter to stand close to the fire.

"I never saw snow like this. I mean it. Never. Do you know, I can't even see my mules down there? They're, what? Thirty feet away? Twenty? I can't see them."

Frank Roderus

"Don't try to go down to them," Cap warned. "You could get lost, even that close. And with the noise this wind is making, we wouldn't hear you if you shouted. Stay here. Later on if you want you can rig a line and tie it to your waist. Let Jack and Clee pay out rope as you go. If you quit moving or they think you're in trouble, they can haul you back up. But give it some time for the snow to compact itself so you won't bog down in it if there's drifts between us and the mules."

"You're sure we'll be all right here?"

Cap waved his hand, indicating the inside of their little pocket of warmth. "We're all right so far, aren't we?"

"Aye, I suppose we are at that. Damnedest thing, the way the fire keeps the cold away."

"We'll be all right as long as we have wood to burn," Cap said.

"And if we run out of wood?"

"Let's just say it would be a whole lot better if that didn't happen, Mr. Magruder."

Clee Brown picked up the coffeepot and went to scoop snow to fill it again. Wood they might eventually run out of, but their water supply was inexhaustible.

Behind Magruder, Jack rolled his eyes and sent a nervous glance out into the curtain of solid white that drew in the limits of the world within arm's length.

Chapter Fifty-five

The snow stopped sometime during the fourth day of the storm. None of them knew exactly when the snowfall dissipated because the continuing winds carried so much of the previously fallen snow that for all practical purposes the whiteout was undiminished. Within hours, though, the airborne density decreased. It became possible to see partially buried treetops north and south of the snug and secure lean to, then for Magruder to peer out and see that his mules were all still huddled, rumps and backs crusted with a thick rime of ice caused by their own body heat, but all of them alive and standing with their muzzles close to the picket rope. The big mulepacker was grinning broadly when he reported the discovery to the others.

"What about down below?" Cap asked. "Can you see across the valley now?"

"Didn't look," Magruder admitted. "Just a minute." He poked his head out into the cut of the wind again, then came back to the fire and hunkered beside it. "Yeah, I can see. But there sure isn't much out there to look at. This side is blown pretty clean, but the whole east slope on the other side of the drainage is covered. So's the bottom. It's full . . . I dunno how deep. The blowdown is covered over complete. Not so much as a stick visible. And some of that timber was, what, ten, twelve feet high when we were working down in it the other day? I'd say the snow at the bottom is at least that deep. Maybe as much as twenty feet." He tried to whistle, but managed to produce only a thin rush of air; his lips were too cold from the brief exposure to the wind for him to properly feel or control them. "We're going to have a terrible time breaking trail for my babies," Magruder said.

Cap looked at him. "I'm going to tell you a hard truth, Mr. Magruder, and you aren't going to like it. But before you get mad at me, stop and think a spell."

Magruder frowned at him. "I don't like the sound of that."

"I told you that you wouldn't. Don't expect you to. But I do expect you to listen to reason, and when you've thought it through, I expect you'll do what you got to."

"Go on, then."

"We're, what, four or five days out from the first camp?"

"Something like that, yes."

"And drifts all the way there, right?"

Magruder nodded.

"You and Jack and Mr. Brown here are strong men, but you can't cut your way through twenty-foot drifts. The mules couldn't break that kind of trail either."

"What are you getting at, Mr. Marsden? Surely you don't think we can sit here and wait out the thaw. That could be a month. Hell, it could be next spring before the last of this melts."

"That's right, Mr. Magruder, it could very well take that long." Cap reached for the coffeepot, but Clee Brown got to it before him and poured a cupful for the old man. Their food supplies were diminished, but not yet to the point of concern, and they still had a world of water available to them and an ample supply of coffee.

Cap took a sip of the belly-warming coffee and looked long and hard at Magruder before he spoke again. "You have to leave your mules behind, mister. We have to go on without them."

Magruder sputtered and began to yelp, but Cap cut him off. "I know how you must feel about that, and I'm sorry. But it has to be done. You said yourself it could be a month or even way longer before we could force a trail for the animals."

"But—"

"We none of us would survive that long. No, let me correct that. If we had to, we'd survive that long. We have wood enough from the blowdown that could be collected again now that the snow's stopped. The wind won't last much longer, and after that it'd be just a matter of sitting and waiting for the trails to become passable again. We'd manage. End up having to eat your mules one at a time until we could walk the rest of them out, but we'd make it. I'd see to that.

"But it would be pointless. We'll go on. Give it another day or two—Lord knows there's plenty enough work that has to be done first so we can move through all this mess—but we'll be fine. It's just that we can't take your mules with us. I'm sorry, but we can't."

"We can't leave them behind, dammit. I won't do that."

207

Cap nodded. "A man has to do what he thinks best, of course. But I think when you've thought this through from one side to t'other you'll see that I'm right. We got to go on. They can't."

"And what is it you say I should do with them?"

"Since we can't take them, you got two ways you could go. One, and it might be the more humane thing in the long run, though there's no way to know that now, the one would be to cut their throats here and now and make sure they don't suffer."

"You know I couldn't do any such thing, damn you," Magruder snapped.

"I do know that, but like I say, it may turn out to be the most humane thing in the long run. Your other choice would be to give them a chance to make it on their own if they're able. Mules are smarter than horses, and even a horse knows enough to paw down through snow to reach grass. It could be that your mules will be able to move far enough to keep themselves going on what little forage they'll find. I personally don't believe there will be enough to feed them all, but I'd be pleased to be wrong about that."

"Just turn them loose and walk away from them?" Magruder sounded aghast at the thought.

"Yes, as a matter o' fact. Let them forage on their own and you come back for them whenever the melt starts. Maybe by then, a month, two, whatever, maybe by then you can gather up however many of them are left and get them out with you. But in the meantime, you have to save Jack and yourself. Clee and me can go on without you if you insist, of course, but that would be a poor decision on your part. After all, man, much as you care for those animals, that's all they are. Animals. You can't put their lives ahead of yours. Or your man's."

"Captain Marsden, sir?" It startled Cap to hear Jack speak. Magruder's helper only rarely uttered a sound and then seldom bothered with actual words. For a time Cap had even thought he was mute. In truth he was dull but not truly dumb, at least not in the literal sense.

"Yes, Jack?"

"I don't wanta stay here e'en if Mr. Ma'ruder does, sir. Can I come with you an' Clee?"

Cap nodded. "The more of us there are when we walk out, Jack, the better it'll be for all of us."

"Walk out," Magruder snorted. "Just how do you think you are going to 'walk' out of here, Mr. Marsden? You and that wheeled chair of yours?"

"Mr. Magruder, Clee and Jack and I will walk away from here, don't you worry. I hope you'll go with us, but of course that's up to you."

Magruder snorted again and turned his back to the old man.

Cap did not bother fretting himself about that. He expected Magruder to resist good sense when he first heard it. But then he also expected the man to come along in two days' time or so when the rest of them would be ready to move. Cap hoped he was right about that. But he and Clee and Jack would go with or without Magruder. Cap had no intention whatsoever of sitting in this isolated valley until the spring melt before he could continue his pursuit of the men who'd murdered Rebecca.

Chapter Fifty-six

The old man was able to contribute more than mere good advice for a change. It pleased him

With Clee bringing him the materials he required, and Jack now pitching in to Cap's direction as well, Cap's hands returned easily to tasks he would have thought long forgotten.

He used new-cut wood, dry and gray to all outward appearances but still green and supple beneath the layers of bark, to bend and form the shapes he wanted. Magruder's nearly endless supply of tough, thin lashing cord taken off the pack frames served as lacing.

Cap could have used strips of green mule hide instead, and indeed they might have been even better because he could have cut them wider than the slender cord.

He rejected that possibility for two reasons. One was that the lashing cord would not stretch with use, while fresh rawhide would have required tightening from time to time. The other was that the loss of one of his beloved mules probably would have broken Magruder's spirit and taken his will to survive along with it. Cap was sure Magruder would join them when the time came. He was equally sure the man would choose to free the mules and give them that slim chance of survival rather than kill them to save them the pain of slow starvation.

At any rate Cap planned for Magruder's presence on the hard, cold trail ahead.

"Are you sure you know what you're doin' there, cap'n?" Clee asked at one point. "What for we need those things?"

"Ever hear of snowshoes, Clee?"

Brown shook his head.

"You fellows who can walk will wear these under your boots. See how I'm making these little harnesslike rigs here? You slide your toe under here. Tie this bit behind your heel and this piece over top of your foot. That holds the thing on. Hard to walk in until you get used to them. They feel strange, and you'll trip all over yourself the first day or so. But what they do is spread your weight wide. They let you walk on top of the snow instead of falling into it. Doesn't matter then how deep a drift is. You walk over the top of it."

Clee looked skeptical of the contraptions Cap was making, but he did not say so.

"How about you, Jack? Have you ever used snowshoes before?"

"Yes, sir. When I was a yonker back home in Vermont. Used them to go to school in the snow time."

"You were a scholar, Jack?"

Magruder's swamper and hey-boy grinned. "Three years of it, I went. Can't cipher very good, but I can read a little. And I can write out my name good enough, by golly, so anybody can read it."

"Good for you, son."

Jack beamed at the words of meager praise and afterward redoubled his efforts to help Cap with whatever the old man wanted.

Cap made six pairs of snowshoes, wanting to be sure there would be spares enough in case of unforeseen difficulty on the trail.

While he was doing that, Clee and Jack were just as busy building a light sled—really more of a sledge—to carry Cap's wheelchair.

The hammock poles that had extended in pairs from mule to mule to transport Cap in one sling and his wheelchair in another were cut into thirds, and half of those cut again into one-sixth the original length.

The remaining longer poles, each of them straight-grained ash that Magruder winced at losing, were laid out to form the longitudinal members of what was to become Cap's sledge. The shorter pieces were lashed in place as crossmembers.

Finally canvas from Magruder's pack covers was stretched tight on the underside of the resulting frame. The canvas, supported by the wooden framework, would ride over the top of the snow.

Cap's chair was tied tight on top of the frame. The old man would ride in it with Clee and Jack on their snowshoes pulling by way of some makeshift harnesses and ropes attached directly to the sledge.

Magruder, Cap figured, could walk ahead, compacting the crust on the snow ahead of the sledge and guiding the others along the way.

Their supplies, what few they could carry, would ride on the sledge behind the chair.

They would take food, coffee already roasted and ground, blankets, tinder, and candles.

Magruder owned a good supply of the newfangled lucifer matches—sputtering, sulfurous, nasty-smelling things that continually amazed and delighted Cap, who had first come to the mountains long before such inventions had made life easier—but no match burns long enough to set alight damp wood. That was where Cap's horde of dry, shaved tinder and the candles would come in. With those at hand, they would never have to face the prospect of a camp without fire.

"I say we're ready," Cap declared the evening of the third day following the storm. "We'll leave at first light. Mr. Brown, I would thank you if you would read aloud to us from your Bible tonight. Something about the chosen being led out into the wilderness, perhaps."

"Yes suh, cap'n, I will surely do that."

Chapter Fifty-seven

It galled Cap to be dragged along like so much baggage, carried forward by dint of other men's muscle and sweat.

He had labored through mountain cold and deep snow himself every winter for years. Waded through ice-rimmed streams from one trap set to another. Cut wood and huddled turtlelike against countless storms. He remembered the sharp, stinging burn of cold air drawn deep into laboring lungs, remembered too the feel of sweat running down his ribs beneath layers of clothing and fur no matter the intensity of the cold, sweat that turned seemingly to ice and sent chills clear in to the bone once the effort ended.

Exhaustion was a constant enemy in bitter cold, and so was a lack of water, brought on both by sweat and the loss of moisture through the mouth in such extreme dry conditions.

Cap insisted that the others keep their heads covered at all times to avoid loss of body heat, and he had the slowly moving procession stop not only at noon, but several times each day.

They stopped long enough to gather wood, warm themselves before a fire, and drink several cups of coffee each time. None of the others seemed to notice, or if they did they offered no comment, but Cap was paying close attention to the effects of the journey on the men, and he increased the number of stops—and his insistence that each man drink plenty of hot beverages—when he realized that despite their intake of fluids, the hard-working men seldom had to eliminate liquids. A man whose body is not producing urine is a man on the edge of trouble.

He never mentioned any of that, though. Aloud he encouraged and praised. Inwardly he cursed himself for his inability to contribute to the terrible effort that was required to pull him and his sledge through the endless miles of snow-clogged trail and over the massive drifts.

On the evening of the second day, Magruder almost tearfully acknowledged that his mules could never have fought their way through conditions like this.

On the evening of the fifth, he announced, "Tomorrow, boys. If we're where I think we are, then tomorrow we should hit Orofino. Mayhap by noon if the way isn't too bad."

It was the news Cap had been wanting. He slipped his hand under the heavy layer of blankets heaped over his lap. The solid, purposeful grip of the Remington revolver was comforting there.

Chapter Fifty-eight

It was past noon, but only a little, when they dragged into Orofino. Literally dragged, with Clee and Jack bending into the reworked mule harness in order to pull Cap on his sled-borne chair.

"I don't know that I've ever been so glad to see a town before this," Magruder said. "Or so anxious to get back out of one again."

"You aren't thinking about turning around and going back out anytime soon, are you?" Cap asked.

"Quick as I think I can get my babies out. I got to. You know that."

"I expect so. About the fee we agreed on for this trip . . ."

"I know. I didn't hold up my end of the deal," Magruder admitted. "I contracted to carry you here, and I couldn't do the job. You don't owe me nothing."

Cap coughed into his fist. "That, um, isn't exactly the way I was looking at it."

"I said you don't owe me, Mister Marsden. But if

216

you think you're entitled to damages, you can just sho—"

Cap laughed. "What I had in mind, sir, is that I pay a fair share toward replacement of the equipment you lost. After all, it was for my benefit that a lot of it was destroyed. Uh, over and above the agreed fee for the transportation, that is. You did get us here." Cap smiled. "In a manner of speaking."

"You don't have to do that."

"Legally, you mean?" The old man shrugged. "I wouldn't know about that. But it's the right thing to do."

Magruder chuckled and extended his hand for Cap to shake. "Captain Marsden." It was the first time Cap could recall him ever using the title. "I apologize for all the things I've been thinking to myself about you ever since we walked off and left my mules back there."

"Just as well then that I don't know what those thoughts were," Cap agreed. "And I accept your apology, sir."

Magruder nodded toward the front of the sledge, where Clee and Jack were taking a breather, both of them with sweat beginning to freeze on their beards. "Mind if I have my man back now? Or aren't you done with him?"

"I'm sure Mr. Brown and I can manage by ourselves from here," Cap said. He motioned for Jack to come closer, then removed one of the bulky but warm blanket-mittens they all had been wearing since the start of the storm. Cap found a twenty-dollar double eagle and gave it to the startled helper. "My thanks go with it," Cap said.

Jack looked confused. But pleased. He did not, Cap noted, make any attempt to refuse the gratuity. But then perhaps Jack was not quite so dull as Cap had initially believed.

"Mr. Brown."

"Yes, cap'n?"

"I believe that's a hotel I see over there. Do you think you can take me to it without Jack's help?"

"I'm sure I can manage that little pull, cap'n."

"Then Mr. Magruder, we bid you good day, sir. If you'd care to drop by the hotel later on, I'd be pleased to buy you a drink, and we can settle our account. How does that sound?"

"More than fair, captain. More than fair."

Chapter Fifty-nine

"You want me to go out and start spreadin' the word, cap'n?"

"What word would that be, Clee?" Cap was seated on the side of a bed. The bed had the thinnest, lumpiest, sourest-smelling mattress he'd ever seen in his long life. At the moment, he considered it to be one of the loveliest articles he'd ever laid eyes upon, and had he had the leisure, he would gladly have spent the next week and a half sleeping off the effects of their recent passage from Virginia City.

"Word about them men, cap'n. The ones you looking for." Clee was nearby, but standing. He hadn't yet gotten up courage enough to trust his bulk to the spindly cot the hotel had brought into the room for him at Cap's insistence.

Cap shook his head. "Not this time, my friend. I learned my lesson about that already. They heard I was looking for them, and they laid an ambush for me." He smiled. "I may be gullible sometimes, Clee, but I'm not completely stupid. This time there won't be any advance warnings broadcast. And this time I know what one of them looks like. Don't forget, I was face-to-face with Art Coffrey. The others snuck up behind, but I'll know Coffrey when I see him again." His expression turned grim. "And I will see that man again, Clee. I guarantee it."

"You think nobody'll notice if'n I wheel you around town, cap'n?"

The old man's anger dissolved into a grin. "Clee, my friend, they'll talk even more when I go walking around with my spare leg. But I'm counting on the fact that Coffrey and his friends won't be warned by that. After all, they think I'm long dead and buried. They have no reason to worry about anyone coming after them. As far as they know, they've gotten clean away with their evil."

"We just gonna go from one saloon to another, cap'n?"

"That's about it, Clee. I intend to go from one likely place to another."

"An' if somebody asks what we doin' here, cap'n?"

It was a question Cap hadn't bothered to think out before, and he was grateful to the big man for asking it now while he had time to come up with a logical excuse.

He pursed his lips and thought for a moment. Looking for a claim to buy might have seemed ordinary enough, but it would not allow for the sort of questions he wanted to ask nor for the right sort of responses.

"I think," he said slowly, talking it out as the germ of an idea began to refine and shape itself in his mind, "I think I'm here looking for my son. I need you to help me get around, of course. My boy . . . hmm, his name is Aaron. Mine will be . . ." He laughed. "I think I'll be Brown. If you don't mind me borrowing your moniker for a little while."

"Does that mean we related now, cap'n?"

Cap got a chuckle out of that too. "Could be, Clee. But we wouldn't admit to that now, would we?"

"No suh, cap'n, I expect not."

"To get back to the point, Clee, I'm here looking for my son Aaron. He, um, he's my only surviving child. He got the gold fever and disappeared last spring. I know he was in Virginia City this past summer, but he was using a false name there."

"I like that," Brown said. "You don' know what he calling himself now so you ask for somebody look like him. Except what you ask about is somebody look like that Art Coffrey fella, is that it?"

Cap grunted and gave a vigorous nod. "Does that sound good to you, Clee?"

"It do, cap'n. Mighty fine. An' do you tell me what this man look like, cap'n, or anything you know about them other two, I slip around an' ask the back room help."

"Pardon me?"

"You know. Ask the po' folk. Bootblacks an' house maids and like that, niggers an' Meskins and whoever else gets kicked an' paid small money." Clee's grin broadened. "Niggers like that see an' hear more'n the quality folk thinks they do, cap'n. Tell you what, whyn't you lay down on that nice bed there and get you some sleep. You look like you gonna fall down do you try an' walk with your spare leg right now anyhow. Get you some rest. I'll go see if there's niggers an' other servants in this here gold camp. If they is, we know real quick about them men you wantin' to find, cap'n. Now you tell me what I should ask for, then you close you eyes. I won't be gone too awful long. When I get back mayhap you know right where to find those mens, cap'n."

Cap considered the offer. He liked it. "All right, Clee. And thank you."

Chapter Sixty

"Hanson's Cafe," Clee said, a huge grin splitting his face in two.

"What's that?" Cap muttered. He was still half-asleep, his nap interrupted by Clee's door-banging arrival.

"The man Arthur Coffrey. He eats most every night at this Hanson place."

"Do you really think . . . ?" It seemed too good to be true.

"Got to be, cap'n. Got to be your man. Him and a partner name of Monk share a claim just nawth o' town. Dirt hole claim, it is. No water. But folks say they bring in a awful lot o' nuggets that are pounded smooth like they come outta water."

"That's the same dodge they used over in Virginia City, isn't it? Buy a worthless claim for pennies so they have a legitimate reason to have gold in their pockets, then steal whatever they can get their hands on from honest men and pass it off as the fruits of their own labor."

"Sho' sound like it to me, cap'n, but this Monk fella that's his partner don't sound like that Shear fella nor the other one you say is called Rayne. Nobody know nothing about them aroun' here, cap'n."

"You're sure of Coffrey, though?"

"Yes suh, cap'n. There's a little old colored gal. She works cleanin' up in a bawdy house. Cute little old gal, but decent. All she does at that place is wash an' like that. She don't see no menfolk, you understand. She know this Coffrey. Mean-tempered, she says. Had to pay the madam woman extra 'cause he beat on a couple o' the working gals there."

"Take a shine to this little colored girl, did you, Clee?" Cap's comment was meant only to be a friendly tease. He was not prepared for the bleak, stricken expression that came onto the big man's usually happy face.

"No suh, cap'n," Clee sputtered. "I'm a married man and a Christian gennelmun—if you'll excuse the expression from a nigger—with a fine lady wife back home and two little girls to keer for."

"Oh, Lord. I didn't know. I'm sorry, Clee. I was only trying to make a joke. A very bad one, I'm afraid. Why didn't you ever tell me you were married?"

"Never saw the need, I expect."

"But I've taken you away from your home, your family. I never even thought about how the travel might affect you or a family."

"Cap'n, my wife, she know I don' fool around. She know I love her an' our babies. An' this here work with you, cap'n, it's the best-paying job I ever been lucky enough to have. I won't lie to you, cap'n. I'd ruther be home with my own. But this job is good. And you a good man." Clee allowed himself a small smile. "For a white man, that is."

Cap laughed just a little, a very little, relieved Clee

did not resent Cap's failure to learn more about this relative stranger upon whom he had come to rely so very heavily.

"I apologize, Clee, and I thank you for being so understanding. I have to thank you for the information too. Now if you'll tell me where this cafe is and help me into my spare leg, there's something I'll be needing to do this evening."

"First off, cap'n, it's awful slippery out there. Lotta ice on the ground. I don't think it's a very good idear for you t'go off by you'self on that spare leg. Better for me to take you in the chair."

Cap thought it over, but only for a moment. Clee knew the conditions outside. And in no way did Cap want to risk a slip and fall that could ruin his chances to come face-to-face with Art Coffrey again.

"You're sure this man Monk isn't one of the others that I'm after, Clee?"

"Pretty sure, cap'n. The gal who tol' me all this say Monk has red hair like a regular ol' carrot. I expect that isn't something you'd've forgot to tell me about them other men."

"No, none of the ones who murdered Rebecca had red hair, I'm afraid. Did your friend say anything about where Shear and Rayne might be now, Clee?"

"Not noplace in Orofino, I expect, or she'd more'n likely know about them."

"Damn it, if they split apart . . ." Cap thought about it for a moment, then shrugged. "I'll just have to ask Mr. Coffrey, won't I?"

"Real polite, cap'n, right?"

"Exactly, Clee. I most definitely want to ask him politely."

"Be all right if'n I rest a little before we go out again, cap'n? Coffrey won't show up to Hanson's till late, they say. He never come in early."

"That'll be fine, Clee." Cap felt bad that he hadn't thought of it himself. After all, the past few weeks, and especially the past few days, had been even harder on Clee than they had been on Cap. Clee was more than entitled to some rest now that they were warm and safe again.

"One thing, though, Clee."

"Yes, cap'n?"

"Don't you ever apologize to me again about calling yourself a gentleman. Or for that matter your wife a lady. You aren't a nigger, you aren't colored, and you're no nigra, neither. You're a friend. All right?"

"Yes suh, cap'n." Clee grinned. "If you say so."

"Go to sleep, Clee."

The big man winked at Cap, then very carefully committed his weight to the rickety cot that had been brought in for him.

The side rails of the collapsible camp cot creaked and sagged, but they held. Within seconds Clee was snoring, the sounds wet and loud inside the confines of the tiny hotel room.

Chapter Sixty-one

"You're welcome here, mister, but your nigra will have to eat out back. I'm sure you understand." The restaurant owner, Hanson presumably, had the slow and easy rhythms of the south in his voice.

Cap considered that for only an instant. And, his right hand happening already to be beneath the lap robe at the moment so as to keep the Remington revolver from being jostled of the chair seat by the bumping and jolting of the wheels, Cap took advantage of the fact and said, "Thank you, sir, thank you, but I'll be needing the help of my man here." He smiled. "Unless you would care to cut my meat and feed me supper. It's a chore he generally does."

Hanson's challenging expression softened. "I apologize, sir. I didn't know."

Cap waved his left hand in dismissal. "Of course you couldn't. 'Course not." He peered over his shoulder at Clee Brown, who hadn't reacted in any way. But then this sort of thing was probably normal to him, although it certainly was not the sort of treatment Cap was accustomed to accept. "Wheel me over to that chair, boy. Sharp now."

"Yes, suh, bossman suh," Clee mumbled. He bobbed his head. Cap thought there was a glimmer of amusement in the big man's dark eyes and perhaps also a small tightening at the corners of his mouth.

"And you, goodman Hanson. I'll be wanting two plates if you please. Can't have my servant here lollygagging in the kitchen by himself after I'm done, you know. I need for him to fill up while I'm at my supper too so his services won't be lost to me after."

"Yes, sir, that will be quite all right," Hanson said.

Cap's left hand fluttered limply to motion Hanson away. Behind his back Cap thought he heard Clee choke back a low, throttled noise.

With that out of the way, Clee wheeled Cap to a table at the far back end of the small cafe, pulled away the stool that was in place there, and wheeled Cap close to the crude table.

The interior of the cafe was already filling up despite the relatively early hour for a supper trade, and no wonder. Whatever Hanson had, or lacked, in manners, the scent of his cooking was almighty good. The place smelled as fine as a farmhouse at Thanksgiving.

Even so, Cap hoped they did not have to sit here stuffing themselves for very long while waiting for Art Coffrey to make an appearance. After all, a man can only hold but so much of even the most tempting foods.

As it turned out, the wait was not long at all.

But then, Cap realized, it was not like Coffrey was such a hardworking man that he would be held long at his labors. No doubt the fellow wanted to get supper out of the way early so he could get to the more interesting pursuits of the evening.

Cap recognized Coffrey the instant the man walked in. There was a red-haired man with him, but Cap's eyes were locked only on Coffrey.

The last time Cap saw this man, Coffrey was busy trying to commit murder.

Another murder, that is.

He had already killed little Rebecca.

The knowledge made Cap's hand tremble as a flush of hatred filled his belly and chest and threatened to squeeze his heart clear up into his throat and gag him.

"You all right, cap'n?" Clee whispered behind Cap's ear.

"Those two who just came in. That's them, Clee. Coffrey is the one in the blue blanket coat. Let them find a place to sit. Then I want you to push me to their table facing Coffrey. Then, Clee, I want you to step clear. You hear me, friend? I want you to step away quick once you put me in front of him."

"Yes, suh. As you say, cap'n."

Coffrey and Monk chose a table toward the front. Cap took in a sharp breath. He wished he could still . . . he shook his head impatiently. It didn't matter a damn what he wished. What counted was not what he wanted, but what was. Right here. Right now.

The two miners—criminals was more like it, Cap thought, although he had no real evidence to that effect against the man named Monk—sat and gave their attention to the menu posted on a chalkboard above Hanson's counter.

"Now," Cap said.

He felt the chair lurch and turn as Clee rolled him swiftly toward the man who had murdered little Rebecca.

Chapter Sixty-two

"Remember me, Coffrey?"

"No, I don't think I do, I—" The man froze, turned suddenly pale.

Cap smiled just a little. "I thought you would."

"But I thought . . ."

"That I was dead? Of course you did. And I almost was. Should have been, for that matter. Surprised to see me, Coffrey? Just a little?"

"Look. Mister. About . . . what happened."

Cap nodded.

"That wasn't my doing. I swear before God it was Tom Rayne and Ev Shear. It was them. I . . . didn't want nothing to do with what they done. That's why we split up. You see they ain't here with me. We split up and they went on alone. Me and Leroy, we have us a little claim. It ain't so much, but it's honest work."

"And back in Virginia City, Coffrey? Was that all their doing too? I seem to remember you starting the shooting that day. I seem to remember you trying to kill me then."

"I . . . what could I do, mister? You was after us. I didn't think you'd sit down and listen to reason. Didn't think you'd believe me if I tried to tell you what really happened that time. Besides, I was more scared of Tom and Ev than I was of some graybeard old man. You know? I'm being honest with you, mister. I'm trying to make you understand."

Cap looked at Monk for the first time. "Are you in this with your partner?"

"Old man, I don't have any idea what this is about. But me and Art are partners. I guess it's share and share alike between us, so if you got a beef with him then you got one with me too."

"Fair enough," Cap said. He raised his voice so men at the tables around them could better hear. They were already listening, Cap was certain. They might as well know the what and the why of it. There would be less chance of interference if they did.

"This man Art Coffrey is one of three who raped and then killed my granddaughter. Rebecca Brenn, her name was. She wasn't but fourteen years old. Scarcely more than a baby. Coffrey and two men, name of Everett Shear and Thomas Rayne, grabbed her on her way to the backhouse in the middle of the night. They carried her off and they abused her terrible bad before they killed her. This was down in Wyoming Territory, and I know for a fact what all they did to her because I'm the one that found the child's body.

"I caught up with them once before over in Virginia City, and Coffrey here stood face-to-face with me while the other two crept up behind like the cowards they all three are and shot me down. Coffrey thought I was dead. They all did. But I'm here to tell you, gentlemen, that I won't die. Not until this man in front of me and Everett Shear and Thomas Rayne are all dead and buried. I won't die until justice has been done for my grandbaby.

"Now what do you say about that, Arthur Coffrey?" Cap pointed an accusing finger into the face of the startled Coffrey.

"He's wrong, boys," Coffrey said quickly. "He's lying."

"He don't sound like a liar to me," one of the men in the cafe said bluntly. "And I'd say it takes a brave man to come into a place all crippled up like he is and demand that justice be done. Mister, can you back up what you say?"

"There are law officers from Omaha to San Francisco who have gotten wanted bulletins naming all three of them," Cap said without taking his eyes off the table before him.

"A shoot-out between grown men is one thing," another voice said, "but doing like that to a kid, a rope is the only answer for that."

"But I'm innocent," Coffrey bleated. "I swear to God, boys, I never had aught to do with the kid. I tried to get the old man off our trail, sure. I admit that. But he said himself I faced him square. It wasn't me tried to shoot him in the back. He said that his own self, boys. You got to listen to me. I'm an innocent man."

"If you're innocent, Arthur Coffrey, you tell me where Shear and Rayne are now," Cap said, his voice still loud and penetrating.

"I don't know where they . . ." Coffrey glanced nervously away from Cap, surveying the mood of the miners who surrounded the table now. "I . . ."

"Are they such good friends you'd be willing to die for them?" one of the miners asked.

"No, I . . . they went down to San Francisco, I think. That's where they said they were going from here. They have a pal there. A saloon keeper. His name is Fon . . . Fom . . . Fromm, that was it. Casey Fromm. He has a saloon. I don't know where exactly. They said I could catch up with them there if I wanted. I don't know no more than that, mister. I swear to you I don't."

"Old man, what do you want done about this one?" someone asked.

"I told you that already. I expect to see him dead for the crimes he committed."

"He claims he didn't do any of that."

"I said he's a murderer," Cap responded. "I never claimed he's stupid. How dumb would a man have to be to sit there and confess to molesting a little girl when there's a roomful of honest men listening to what he says?"

"We won't let murder be done in our town," one of the miners said. "We don't countenance that."

"Is a fair fight considered murder here?" Cap asked.

"Hell, of course it ain't. But there couldn't be no fair fight. I mean, hell, mister, you're crippled. Only got the use of one hand. Already got to be pushed around in that contraption. How could you take on an able man with the use of both his hands? I don't see how that could be."

"But if I'm willing, friend?"

"Then I would have to say that you're crazy, old man."

Cap shrugged. "Nevertheless . . ."

"If that's what you want, mister, we none of us here would try to gainsay you."

"Arthur Coffrey," Cap said firmly, "I say you are a liar, a murderer, and worse. I challenge you to face me if you deny the charges I lay against you."

Art Coffrey began to look a whole lot happier. He pushed his chair back from the table and stood. The grip of a large pistol was visible sticking out of the waistband of his trousers.

"You stupid old son of a bitch," Coffrey snarled. His right hand began to move.

Chapter Sixty-three

The front of Cap's lap blanket billowed forward ahead of a lance of pale yellow flame, and the room was filled with the earsplitting roar of a large-caliber gunshot fired indoors.

Coffrey was startled into immobility, his hand poised with fingers extended but not quite touching the walnut grips of his pistol.

"Damn you, you've shot me," he exclaimed in a voice of doubt and wonder.

Cap confirmed the opinion by doing it again. This time he withdrew his right hand from beneath the woolen lap robe, took careful aim, and sent a second bullet into Art Coffrey's body, after which he used the palm of his left hand to extinguish the small fire that threatened to flare up in his lap.

Coffrey staggered half a step back, stopped there, and peered down at his shirtfront, where a bright scarlet stain was quickly spreading.

"Not me. No sir, mister, not me." The words came from Coffrey's partner Leroy Monk, who had come

234

halfway off his chair only to stop there in mid-motion. The man was staring intently past Cap's right shoulder.

Cap turned his head to see a small, slightly rusty four-shoot gambler gun in Clee's big hand. The little pistol was pointed unerringly at Monk's belly button.

"I . . . I told you fellas, I ain't a party to this, not none of it," Monk stammered. He blinked several times, then gave his gut-shot former partner a baleful look and hurried past Coffrey and out onto the street.

Cap returned his attention to Coffrey, whose knees began to sag as the blood drained from him and across the front of his trousers so that it looked like he had soiled himself. And in all probability, Cap knew, the man had done that too. It was a common enough reaction to a mortal wound, and Cap had seen more of those in his day than he'd ever wanted.

This one, though, this one pleased him.

The old man watched with grim satisfaction as the life's blood seeped out of Coffrey's body and as a waxy pallor crept into his flesh.

Just that quickly, the stubble of unshaven whiskers stood out in bold contrast against the dying man's chin and neck, and his eyes began to glaze.

Cap was mildly impatient with Rebecca's murderer. Coffrey swayed, braced his feet wide apart, and managed to remain on his feet a few seconds longer.

He looked down at the pistol butt in his waistband, then back up at the old man who had killed him. His hand moved feebly in the direction of the gun once more.

Cap raised his revolver, sighted with care, and directed a final ball into Coffrey's forehead.

The killer's head snapped back and for a moment was surrounded by a misty red halo as moisture spraying from the exit wound caught the lamplight in Hanson's Cafe.

Coffrey's head snapped back, and this time he dropped.

Cap watched the man fall, then slowly and methodically he began to reload the .44 Remington.

"I thought you said you couldn't use your right hand, mister," one of the miners complained, as if the fact were somehow unfair.

Cap gave the spectator a cold look. "Implied it, maybe. Didn't say it. You got a problem with that, friend?"

"I . . . no, sir. I got no problem with it."

"Mr. Brown, I'd appreciate it if you'd push me back to our table. I see the gentleman brought our supper while we were busy over here."

No one, Cap noticed, complained this time about a black man eating at the same table as a white.

Chapter Sixty-four

The *Petrel II* wallowed sluggishly on a following sea, the stubby bowsprit of the old boat waving back and forth like an aged and weary bird dog looking for game. Cap shivered and tried to huddle deeper into the wraps of blanket that covered him and his chair.

Clee had found a way to keep the chair from rolling hither and yon on the always damp decking. He'd tied the contraption in place against a wooden fitting of some sort—Cap had no idea what purpose the rail-like arrangement served—that wrapped around the forwardmost mast.

That kept the chair secure, but it did nothing to block the cold that soaked all the way down to Cap's bones.

It was funny, the old man reflected, that the numbing cold of the storm in Idaho had not made him anywhere close to this miserable. Now, though, the damp salt air seemed to drive this lesser cold past all the blankets he could pile onto himself, past them and through his flesh, to chill him clear down to the core.

The sensible thing, he supposed, would have been to remain belowdecks in the confinement of the cubicle that passed for a cabin on the little ship.

But that was even worse than the cold he suffered on deck. The cabin was confiningly small and made him feel as if he were in a coffin, just waiting for the sea to cover and claim him.

It stank down there too. The accumulated stench of year upon year of unimaginable cargoes, of badly preserved fish and rotting garbage and bilgewater, all mingled together to form a fetid, noxious stench that made Cap's stomach churn and threaten to erupt at the next lurch or roll of the creaking hull.

The only thing that kept his stomach under some semblance of control was when he was on deck and could see the horizon. Down below, he quickly became disoriented and woozy, so he had Clee carry him up the ladder to his chair at first light and remained there until the night cold drove him unwillingly back into the cabin. He would have slept in the chair if he could have stood the cold throughout the hours of darkness.

Surely, though, they would soon reach San Francisco.

Five days, six at the most, the captain told him when they booked passage back in Oregon. An easy run down the coast to the city of hills, the captain said.

Six days. Right. They had been at sea eight days already, never out of sight of land, at least during daylight, and their progress was so slow Cap was convinced he could still see the same landmarks that had caught his attention when they left port at the start of the voyage.

He could have walked the distance more quickly, he was convinced.

If he could walk.

"Clee."

"Yes, cap'n?"

"Go ask the captain . . ." Cap's voice trailed away into silence, and his shoulders slumped. "Never mind, Clee."

"I'll go ask him, cap'n," Clee said with a broad smile. "It won't be long now. I'm sure it won't."

Cap sighed. When they got ashore, if they ever got ashore, he would have to clean and oil the revolver, he reminded himself, and it probably would be a good idea to buy dry ammunition too. He did not know if these brass self-contained cartridges were as sensitive to moisture as loose powder. Perhaps not. But he did not want to take any chances. If the cartridges were available in San Francisco, he would buy some. If not, well, he would just have to trust to luck and press on ahead.

Chapter Sixty-five

The view from the room was not exactly inspiring. As far as Cap could see, San Francisco Bay consisted largely of mud and rotting wood, the wood being what remained of the hulls of ships abandoned years ago to sink slowly deeper and deeper into the mud.

Cap had little experience with seas or seashores, so he did not know if the dank odor came from the mud that was exposed at low tide or if it was from the dozens, perhaps hundreds of decaying ships. What he was sure of was that this stink colored his perceptions of San Francisco on this first visit to the city.

Cap's previous experience with California, what little of it there had been, consisted of a single winter's visit far to the south, in a country praised by the wide-roving boys in Jedediah Smith's brigade who were the first of the mountain men to cross the Sierra Nevadas. Cap hadn't minded the country all that much at the time, but the Mexicans who governed then were not to his taste in the slightest. He'd spent that one winter there and had felt no desire to return again afterward. He would have felt none now either, save for the hope of finding Rayne and Shear here.

He looked angrily around the small room where he found himself trapped and therefore grumpy.

The room did not please him at all, but it was the only one he had been able to find close to the wharf district, where the bulk of the city's low-class saloons could be found. And Cap assumed that any friend of Thomas Rayne or Everett Shear would be one low-class son of a bitch, so this was where the search for Casey Fromm should likely begin.

Still, he did not like it. The problem was that the room was on the second story of an inn and common house. In order to reach it—or leave it—Cap had to rely on Clee Brown's strong arms to carry him up or down.

It rankled Cap to know that even so small a task as going to breakfast meant being picked up and carried by someone else.

If nothing else, dammit, it was embarrassing. Patrons in the dark, cellarlike public room looked at him with undisguised curiosity whenever Clee moved through the place with Cap cradled in his arms like some oversized, overaged infant.

Compounding that was the lesser nuisance of knowing that even when he reached the privacy of their rented room, Cap still had no freedom of mobility because the wheeled chair that he had come to depend on would not fit through the narrow stairwell leading to the second story, and the old man was not nearly adept enough with the spare leg to manage a long staircase. Once put into place, on the bed or on the small chair set beside the window, Cap was stuck there until Clee moved him again.

Cap fretted and fumed about it, but there was no solution save for him to wait.

He did not even know how long he would have to wait, because shortly after making sure Cap was as comfortable as he was likely to become, Clee had excused himself, saying there were some errands he needed to run if Cap wouldn't mind.

Mind? Of course he minded. But he did not say so aloud. If Brown wanted some time to himself he was more than entitled to it. Cap was already indebted to the man more than he could ever hope to repay. It would have been unconscionable to deny a simple request for free time now.

So Cap sat and stared out across the foul-smelling mud flats and chewed nervously at the inside of his cheek.

San Francisco. It was a city he could come to hate with scarcely any provocation. Or perhaps it was only his own frustration that he so hated. No matter. He wanted this over with. He wanted to see justice done and Rebecca's murder avenged while he still had breath in his body and a hand steady enough to pull a trigger.

But damn them anyway. Damn them all, the two still living and the one already dead. Damn them to the fires of Hell.

Cap peered off across the flats, wet and shining in the sunlight, but the images in his mind had nothing to do with ships or water. All he could see there were the shadowy, as yet formless faces of Thomas Rayne and Everett Shear.

Soon, he prayed, soon he would know them. Soon.

Chapter Sixty-six

"That Mr. Fromm's place, cap'n, it's not real far from here. Couple, three blocks maybe."

"Have you seen it?"

Brown nodded. "I went in, cap'n. Had me a beer there."

"You didn't have any trouble?"

"No suh, cap'n. Lots o' sailors there. White, brown, 'nother black man. They don' care, long as a man's money's the right color."

"Tell me about it, please."

"Not much different from what's downstairs here, cap'n. They mostly sell beer. Got a couple rooms upstairs an' a couple scrawny women take care o' the tables an' I'd say spend some time in them rooms too, but I don' rightly know that for sure."

"Did you see . . . you didn't ask about Shear and Rayne, did you?"

"No suh, cap'n. You said I shouldn't call no 'tention to myself. Just had me one beer an' left. That's all I done."

"You did exactly right, Clee." Cap sighed. "I owe you so much . . ."

It was true, of course, and then some. He depended on Clee Brown in ways he never would have thought to lean on any human, not even wife or close family.

Clee carried him up and down the stairs. Pushed the wheeled chair. Helped him in and out of the spare leg whenever needed. Even helped him get on and off the damned thunder mug.

The man even stood there with a gun in his hand back in Idaho when he thought Art Coffrey's partner might be wanting to take an interest in things.

Cap had never spoken to Clee about that. But he hadn't forgotten it either. He owed this man more than it would ever be possible for him to repay.

And now he was asking Clee to stay with him and support him all the more.

Cap looked at the big black man for several long moments, then cleared his throat and looked away. "They serve food at this place of Fromm's?"

"They do, cap'n."

"Then I'll ask you to take me there for dinner tonight."

"Whatever you say, cap'n."

"Clee."

"Yes, suh?"

"You're a praying man, aren't you?"

"Every day o' my life since the day I was born the secon' time, cap'n."

"Will you pray for me then, please? Before tonight?"

"Cap'n, suh, I don' rightly know is it right to pray for any man's death. I don't expect I could come right out an' do that. But I been prayin' for you, suh, right regular since the day you an' me first met."

"I . . . didn't know that, Clee."

A broad grin split the big man's face. "You ain't the one as has to, cap'n."

"No, I suppose not. It's all right for me to thank you though, I guess."

"Oh, that be fine, suh. But better if you goes right to the source. You know?"

Cap nodded. Then he began cleaning the .44 caliber Remington before reloading it with the fresh cartridges Clee had found for him somewhere in San Francisco earlier in the day.

This might not, he suspected, be the best time to be asking favors of anyone whose entire being was supposed to be devoted to peace and love.

He would think about that part of it later. After he'd found Everett Shear and Thomas Rayne.

Chapter Sixty-seven

Clee was right. Casey Fromm's Owyhee Inn was very much like the place where they had taken rooms. It was dark and shabby, with sawdust on the floor that should have been replaced months ago and a pervading scent of stale beer and sour urine. At that, though, it smelled better than their own small room, if only because it was farther from the waterfront and suffered less from the stink of the mudflats.

A little light was admitted by way of the open doorway leading onto the street outside, but there were no windows to bring any sense of cheeriness inside, and Fromm apparently was too cheap to burn valuable lamp oil during the daytime.

Cap noticed there was nothing breakable in view. No glasses, no mirrors, no pictures in frames that could be grabbed, stolen, or flung at obstreperous patrons.

Once his eyes adjusted to the dim interior of the saloon, he saw that someone had daubed paint on one of the rough-hewn walls in a shape that approximated that of a ship at sea in a storm. The opposite wall contained an even cruder painting of a woman who seemed all hair, thighs, and bare breasts.

The wall painting was a far cry from the pair of slatterns who roved from table to table in the place. Both of them looked like women who had spent forty or more remarkably difficult years on this earth and who held out little hope for future improvement above their current low state. They had limp hair, gray complexions, and empty eyes. Neither of them provided much of a testament about the glowing opportunities available in their particular field of employment.

Cap noticed that neither of them bothered to give him much in the way of attention, although the taller and leaner of the two did send a brief look of appraisal in Clee's direction before concentrating her attentions on a burly, brown-skinned man who spoke a language Cap was positive he had never heard before. He gathered that the bawd did not speak any more of the tongue than Cap did, but that did not deter either her or her potential customer.

Clee wheeled Cap to a table in the far back corner of the place without having to be told, then motioned for the shorter waitress to join them.

"What d'you want, then?" the woman demanded with no warmth or welcome in her voice.

"How's the food here?"

"Hot. You want good and fancy I know some real fine places up toward the Hill."

Cap had no idea what or where she was talking about. "What do you suggest, miss?"

"We got stew or we got soup. The soup is last week's stew with more water added."

He wasn't sure if she was kidding or not, but decided not to ask, just in case the woman was serious. "We'll have the stew."

"Two bowls?"

"If we want more, we'll ask for it later."

"I meant d'you want some for your nursemaid there." Her choice of wording was better than it might have been, Cap conceded.

"We do. And tea if you have it."

"Coffee do instead?"

"Coffee will be fine."

"Stew is two bits a bowl. The coffee's thrown in free."

"Thanks."

"Sure. Whatever you say." She turned and stalked away with a flip of her skirts.

Clee helped Cap to a comfortable position at the table, then seated himself to one side so the old man would have an unobstructed view of the doorway. Clee appeared to be amused by something. Cap did not ask what.

Chapter Sixty-eight

"Cap'n, I hate to say it, but this here plan o' yours ain't working," Clee said as he placed the old man onto the bed back in their own room.

"You're just complaining because you don't like the food over there," Cap accused with a grin.

"Lordy, that's the natural truth," Clee said, making a sour face.

The food at the Owyhee Inn, Cap had to admit, was only marginally edible. He had once had to dine on a soup made of boiled muskrat pelts, the least valuable of the furs being the first to go into a communal pot when hunger demanded such a harsh measure. In his opinion, the boiled muskrat skins were easier on the palate than Casey Fromm's stews. Only a little better perhaps, but even so. . . .

And they had been eating it on a regular basis for three days now, with no sign of either Rayne or Shear.

"You know better than to ask me to give up," Cap said.

"That ain't what I had in mind, cap'n."

"You've really been thinking about this, haven't you?"

"Yes suh, cap'n, I have for a fact."

"I'm willing to listen if you have any ideas."

"Well, suh, what I got to worryin' over is what's gonna happen when those men come in an' see you sittin' there big as life. They both of them gonna go for they guns, cap'n. Two against one. That be bad enough, but what if you lookin' the other way when they come in? What if they get the jump on you? Shoot you down dead before you know they even there. What happen then, cap'n?"

"It isn't something I'm willing to let happen, Clee."

"No, suh, of course you isn't. But what if you got no choice about it? You wind up dead on the floor in that place, there won't be nobody to see justice done for that little girl."

Cap sighed. And silently conceded the truth of what Clee warned him about.

The possibility of failure had been bothering him too, particularly since yesterday afternoon. One of San Francisco's police officers had come into the Owyhee in the middle of the afternoon and, bold as brass, went to the bar, downed a free beer, and accepted a quantity of gold coin from Fromm.

Cap had no idea what the payoff was for, but the mere fact that it happened spoke volumes about the sort of people who frequented the Owyhee and about those who ran it. Obviously this was not a place where justice and decency were held in high regard.

If it came down to that—and it was something he had thought out but had never spoken aloud to any living soul—Cap would willingly have traded his own murder in exchange for hangman's nooses around the necks of Thomas Rayne and Everett Shear. He hadn't so very many years left to him under the best of circumstances, and however many days remained to him would surely be pain-filled thanks to his first encounter with Rebecca's killers. His one life for the two of theirs was a swap he would gladly make.

But the truth was that if he died in a shoot-out at the Owyhee, he felt fairly sure the two friends of Casey Fromm would suffer no retaliation at the hands of the law in San Francisco.

Even in the unlikely event that the police here would bother investigating to begin with, it seemed certain that Fromm and his employees would lie as a favor to their friends.

Justice was not something Cap believed he could trust to anyone other than himself.

"Is there something you have in mind, Clee? Some particular plan?"

"No suh, cap'n. It's just . . . I been watchin' what goes on in that place over there. Payin' attention to the sort of folks that goes there, you know? They worries me, they do."

Cap nodded. He most surely understood. The patrons of the Owyhee Inn were a disreputable lot, and more than once he'd had the idea that if it had not been for the presence of a formidably large attendant at his back, Cap might well have found himself the victim of robbery, assault, or worse at the hands of his fellow diners.

Cap sighed. "I wish I knew what I could do, Clee. But I just don't. I'm sorry, but I don't."

Chapter Sixty-nine

"What d'you want, nigger?" The distaste apparent in the man's voice did not prevent him from accepting Clee's dime in exchange for a glass of weak, tepid beer. Clee noticed that Fromm did not bother adding the nickel's change that he had coming for the beer.

"I'm lookin' for a couple fellas," Clee told him.

"You? Or the old man you been coming in here with?"

"The old man's taking his nap. He don't need to know nothing about me bein' here. You know?"

Fromm gave him a suspicious look, then grunted and looked away to mop at the scarred surface of his bar with a rag that replaced one sort of moisture with another rather than drying the rings and spills he found there.

"Fella up in Idaho tol' me to look for these friends o' his if I had somethin' good goin' an' needed me some help."

"These men you're looking for. They got names, do they?"

"Tom Rayne. Ev Shear. Man I done some business with back in Idaho, his name is Coffrey. Call himself Coffee sometimes. I don' know his right name. Just that."

"Why do anything to help you, nigger?"

" 'Cause when I do find these men, I'm gonna tell them if it's too late an' you done cut them outta a good thing."

"What good thing are you talking about?" Fromm demanded.

"Something too good t'tell the likes o' you," Clee returned. "You think I'm that dumb I blab what I know all around this city? I ain't that dumb, mistuh."

"Why d'you think I'd know anything about these two? What if I never heard of them?"

Clee shrugged. "Coffee, he say if I'm in San Francisco an' have somethin' going that I can't handle by my own self, I oughta come to this here place. Say his friends is friends o' your'n too, so I ought to ask you about them. If you never heard o' them, then I expect this man Coffee done tol' me wrong. I won't bother you no more nor bring the old man in here no more neither. I'll go lookin' elsewhere fo' what I need."

"Is it hard men you're looking for? I might have some friends who could help you out."

Clee gave him a cold look. "It be Ev Shear and Tom Rayne I lookin' for. Don't you worry none. I find them some other way." He drained his beer and wiped a mustache of suds from his upper lip. "I won't be wanting no refill, mistuh, so I take my nickel now if it's all the same to you."

Fromm spread his hands wide and smiled broadly. "Whoa, now. I was just thinking out loud. It could be that I do know the fellows you're looking for. Mind, I'm not saying that I do. But if I could find them . . . what would be in it for me?"

"I'd thank you real nice. That sound good enough?"

"I would think you'd be grateful enough to—"

"Grateful enough to not reach acrost there, mistuh, an' see could I squeeze that pimple on top o' your neck. An' if you think you or the rest o' this pissant crowd be big enough to keep me from doin' it, then I expect we gonna have us some fun findin' out who right an' who wrong about it," Clee said with an eager grin.

"Can you come back here tonight about nine, maybe ten o'clock?"

"The old man don't always sleep good. I sneak out if I can, but it won't be till real late if'n at all."

"I'm not saying I know the men you asked about, mind. But if I happen to talk to them, well, I'm not making any promises. It might be better if I could tell them what it is you'd be wanting their help with."

"Just let me have my nickel, mistuh. Maybe I be back tonight, maybe I don't."

Fromm reluctantly laid a nickel on the bar. Clee thanked him with exaggerated politeness, touched his forehead, and backed several feet away from the bar before turning his back on Fromm and walking out of the Owyhee Inn.

Chapter Seventy

Clee peered into the shadows that surrounded the rickety table in a dark corner of the Owyhee, then glanced suspiciously at Casey Fromm, who was busy behind his bar and too far away to overhear anything that was said. Then he returned his attention to the two men who were hunched over mugs of brandy-laced beer on the other side of the small table.

"The reason I got to do it this way," he explained patiently, "is 'cause I be what you might call conspicuous. You know?"

Tom Rayne nodded. His chum Shear did not bother, just sat there waiting with no apparent sign of interest beyond the contents of his glass.

"That's why I had to get outta Orofino up there in Idaho. Me an' Coffee, we had a pretty good thing goin', us an' a red-headed guy name of Monk. We was doin' all right, but I got seen a couple times. Not so many up there looks like I does." Clee cackled and looked around again to make sure no one was close enough to hear.

255

"I caught on with this rich old fart. Push him here, take him there, pick his scrawny old ass up an' carry him wherever he say. Next thing you know he be wanting me to wipe his ugly white butt for him."

"Rich, you say?" Shear asked.

"Rich enough, yeah. Carries it in a belt inside his britches. I see it all the time. Picked it up an' moved it more'n once too. It's plenty heavy, I'm tellin' you."

"How heavy?"

"Heavy enough we split it three ways, we all be smiling after," Clee said. "I could knock the old bastard in the head when he asleep an' take it all fo' myself except like I already tol' you, they just ain't so many men around that look like me. I, what you call, stand out from the crowd. You know?"

"Go ahead. We're listening."

"Thing is, all kinds o' folks seen me with the old man. If he wind up dead and I ain't around, first thing they do they put out those tellygraph messages. John Law all over the damn country be grabbin' up every big, tall nigger this side of Africa. I figure what I got to do is hang behind an' be the one shout the alarm 'bout the old man bein' robbed an' killed."

"Killed, did you say?"

"It's the safest way. If you too squeamish to do it yourselfs . . ."

"No, I just wanted to make sure that's what you intended."

"That be the safest thing, don't you think?"

"Yes, of course. You say you'll stay behind afterward?"

" 'At's right. Figure one of you can whomp me one, like on the side o' the head. Break the skin there, it bleed something terrible. That'd look real pitiful when someone come to see. I can say there was, oh, four, five guys. Give descriptions an' everything. Say I was knocked out. Woke up to find the old man dead an' the money belt gone. Hide my part of it in my bag. No one think to look there. No one think about a colored man havin' no gold on him. They won't look through my stuff. Not with me all bloody an' upset how my bossman been killed by them terrible men what bonked me an' left me for dead too."

"You wouldn't mind if one of us hit you a lick?"

"Be for the best. Otherwise the coppers, they'll wonder why I ain't hurt an' my bossman dead."

Rayne nodded. "It sounds all right. When do you want to do it?"

"Tonight. Right now. I'm game."

Shear gave Rayne a look of warning, then jerked his head to motion the other man away from the table. "We'll talk this over in private if you don't mind and be right back."

Clee nodded. He looked at the beer he'd been given earlier but had not touched. He didn't intend to drink from it now either. Not that he didn't trust his new partners. Of course not. He just wasn't very thirsty at the moment.

The two remaining murderers of Rebecca Brenn returned to the table minutes later.

Both of them were smiling broadly.

Chapter Seventy-one

Cap hurt. The straps holding his spare leg in place felt like they had been shrinking over the past . . . how long? One hour? Two? He couldn't tell, and did not want to light a lamp so he could see his watch. What he did know for sure was that the straps were beginning to feel as unyielding as iron and as tight as a tire shrunken into place around a new wheel.

That was bad enough, but what was worse was that his left leg had fallen asleep. It was hard enough trying to maintain one's balance in the contraption. If his sound right leg also began to go numb he would surely tumble to the floor. Yet he did not dare move around the tiny upstairs room. The sound of the spare leg striking the flooring like a one-legged man's peg would surely carry downstairs.

Cap settled for fidgeting and muttering and moving about as much as he was able without lifting the tip of the spare leg off the floor.

He stood upright for a time, then leaned against the wall, then pushed himself upright again. He did not want to risk becoming unbalanced, but he had to move enough to remain able to move—and quickly—if the need arose.

For the thirtieth time, or the fortieth perhaps, he touched the walnut grips of the revolver that was tucked inside his waistband. Reassured that the gun had not shifted position, he once again wiped his hands along the seams of his trousers to insure that his palms were dry. He flexed his fingers, alternately making fists and then splaying his fingers wide. He tried taking long, slow breaths. Closed his eyes tight. Rolled his head from side to side in an effort to relax taut neck muscles. Raised first one arm and then the other. Touched the butt of the gun again. It was where it should have been.

How long had it been now, he wondered. How much longer would it yet be? For that matter, was there any real reason why he should continue to stand here in the dark silence?

As a younger man, Cap had participated in half a hundred battles, but he'd never felt this nervous on those few occasions when he'd had time to anticipate them.

But then those fights had not had nearly so much riding on their outcome.

Back then the only thing on the line was Cap's own scalp.

This, tonight, was far, far more important to him.

Chapter Seventy-two

Clee Brown looked carefully around the common room of the silent, sleeping inn. He saw and heard no one. Satisfied that the owner and the other guests were asleep for the night, Clee turned and, placing a finger to his lips, motioned the others inside.

Quiet as ghosts, Tom Rayne and Everett Shear slipped inside and pulled the door shut behind them. Shear, the taller of the two, made sure the latch was not set, that the door would open to a touch if need be.

Clee waited for Shear's nod, then guided the way to the staircase. He pointed to the wheeled chair that sat at the foot of the steps, then pointed upward to show whose device it was. But then, both Rayne and Shear would already know that. Clee was sure they would have picked Casey Fromm's brain for every detail of the probable victim before they ever agreed to meet with Brown back at the Owyhee.

Keeping his big feet close to the wall so as to minimize the likelihood of making a loose tread squeak, Clee slowly climbed the stairs and stopped outside the door to the old man's room.

He motioned toward the door and reached into a pocket for a folding knife.

Rayne shook his head and pushed Clee's hand down, then produced a much larger knife of his own, a slim and lethal stiletto with sharp edges on both sides of a blade that was at least six inches long.

Shear crowded close and took out what looked like a heavy-bladed skinning knife.

In a soft whisper, Clee said, "The bed's straight ahead. He be sleepin' there."

"Does he have a gun?"

Clee nodded. "It's on the dressing table under the window to the right when you open the door. I don' think he can reach it without help, though."

"You go first," Rayne hissed.

Clee nodded again, and silently twisted the doorknob.

He took a deep breath, let half of it out, and then pushed inside the small room.

Rayne and Shear rushed in at his heels, bulling past him in a swift but barely audible charge for the lumpy shape that filled the bed directly in front of them.

There was little light in the room, but a slanting shaft of moonlight flashed sporadically as two knives bit and stabbed again and again and again.

Clee could hear muffled grunts of effort as the two assassins labored at their deadly task.

The knives drove hard and deep into the form on the narrow bed.

Clee Brown eased the door shut at his back and pushed the bolt closed to lock it there.

Chapter Seventy-three

"What the hell's wrong here, Tommy? Why ain't this old bastard wiggling?"

Clee Brown struck a sulfur match. The sudden flare of light illuminated the room, and the light grew stronger when Clee applied the flame to the wick of a wall lamp. The room filled with light, and the would-be murderers saw what surely must have seemed an apparition standing tall and straight in a corner of the room.

"What the . . . ?"

"Back from the dead," Cap growled. "Come back to take you with me."

"The hell you say."

"Do you remember me?"

"I never seen you before in my life," Rayne said. He looked down at the bed, where he and his partner had just successfully killed two pillows and a mound of blankets. Feathers from the tattered pillows drifted off the side of the bed and onto the wooden floorboards.

"Who are you and what the hell are you up to?" Shear demanded.

"You really don't remember me, do you?" Cap asked.

"You heard the man," Shear said. "He never seen you before. Neither have I."

"Think real hard. First there was the little girl. You abused her and then murdered the child to cover yourselves. That was down in Wyoming Territory."

"No, we never—"

"Then there was the incident in Montana. Is it coming back to you now? I caught up with you in Virginia City, but I made the mistake of talking too much about who you were and what you'd done. You found me on the street, you and your friend Art Coffrey. You thought you killed me that day. You were wrong."

The color drained out of Rayne's face as he realized who the old man was. "You're dead!" he blurted.

"No," Cap said mildly. "But you're fixing to be." Slowly, in no rush about it at all, he reached for the Remington in his waistband.

Neither of the murderers bothered wasting time in argument, nor were they foolish enough to attempt to counter a revolver with their knives. Instead they snatched quickly at their own pistols.

Shear was fast. Cap had to give the man credit for that. He was quick as a striking rattlesnake as he plucked a revolver out of a holster concealed beneath his arm.

The gun roared, filling the room with the sound of its explosion and with the stink of burnt powder.

Cap took his time responding. As calmly as if he were back on the banks of the Missouri, practicing shooting clods of earth, he took careful aim and, before Everett Shear had time to trigger a second shot, placed a bullet into the hollow at the base of Shear's throat. The man staggered, turned, and fell loudly to the floor.

Rayne, wide-eyed in disbelief, stood with his own pistol drawn halfway out of its holster. He gaped at his fallen comrade, then looked up in desperation at Cap, who had methodically cocked the Remington and was taking deliberate aim at the bridge of Thomas Rayne's nose.

"I . . . mister, I . . ." Beads of sweat gathered on Rayne's forehead and at his temples. He began to tremble and shudder. He jerked spasmodically and threw his pistol away from him. The gun struck the bed where moments ago Rayne and Shear so gleefully thought they'd killed a man. The gun bounced once and lay there, easily within reach if Rayne wanted to try for it, but he kept his eyes well away from it.

"I ain't armed, mister. I surrender." Rayne shoved his hands toward the ceiling and sidled as far away from the gun as he could manage without tumbling out the second-story window.

"You surrender," Cap repeated.

"That's right, mister. I ain't armed, and I surrender to you." Rayne gave Clee Brown an imploring look. "You're my witness, mister. I give myself up."

"Did Rebecca surrender to you?" Cap asked.

"The kid? I . . . that wasn't me, mister. I swear t'God that wasn't me. It was Ev and Coffee done those things to the kid. I never touched her."

"Funny, but that's what Coffrey said too. Just before I killed him," Cap told him.

"But I'm telling you the truth. Look, I'll make a deal with you. I'll tell the law the whole thing. I . . . I'll even say I was a part of it. I'll testify against the others."

"The others are both dead."

Rayne looked at Clee. "You got to help me. Jeez, you . . . you set this up, didn't you? You was in on this with him, wasn't you?"

Clee nodded. "Every step of the way," he admitted.

"But I've give up now. You got to see that. I've give up and I'll admit to what I done. I'll take whatever the judge says. I will, I swear it."

"The one who's going to judge you won't be sitting in any court of law," Cap said. "And the place you'll be consigned to isn't prison, but everlasting fire."

"You can't . . . it isn't your place to judge. The book says that too, don't it? It ain't for you to judge."

Cap frowned. "You know, that's true. It isn't for me to judge you."

Rayne seemed to relax just a little. He even tried to force a pleading, pitiful look, as if in an appeal for sympathy.

"All I'll do," Cap said, "is send you to face the one who will do the judging."

"No, you can't, I—"

Before Rayne had time to say any more, the Remington bellowed a second time, and Thomas Rayne's head was snapped backward as if by invisible wires.

Chapter Seventy-four

Off to the east, a plume of dark smoke lifted off the winter-brown floor of the desert. That would be the Union Pacific work train approaching end-of-track.

Cap uncapped his bottle and offered it first to Clee, then helped himself to a belly-warming nip.

"You still the be-darnedest white man I ever did see, cap'n, not wiping the neck of that bottle or nothing."

"And you are still a mighty good man, Clee Brown, of whatever color."

"I take that kindly, coming from a man like you, cap'n."

"I meant it kindly."

"Mistuh George, he be on that train a-coming?"

"I expect he will be. His wire said he would meet us here and take us the rest of the way back to Omaha." Cap smiled. "Are you anxious to see your family again?"

Clee grinned. "No more'n a drownin' man's anxious for a breath o' fresh air."

"I won't be staying on in Omaha, you know."

"No, suh, I'd expect not."

"It won't be easy for me when I get home to Santa Fe, though. It'll all be different now, what with this chair and everything."

"Yes, suh, I'd say that be likely."

"I'll be needing help."

"Yes, suh."

"I . . . I'm not a poor man, Clee. And my home is large enough to hold a lot of children."

Clee looked puzzled. "You thinkin' of marrying again, cap'n?"

Cap laughed. "What I was thinking, Mr. Brown, is that there's room in my house for you and your wife and daughters. You'd be welcome. And well-compensated too, for that matter."

"I don' know . . ."

"I wouldn't expect an answer until you've had a chance to talk it over with your wife," Cap told him. Then, smiling, he added, "And until I've had a chance to talk with her too, of course."

"You fixin' to pressure me into takin' you up on what you want, cap'n?"

"I am for a fact, Mr. Brown, I am for a fact."

Off in the distance, Cap could hear the shrill yowl of a train whistle. He tugged the buffalo robe higher under his chin and thought about the journey yet to come. When they reached Omaha, he would be able to visit Rebecca's grave.

Alone. There were things he wanted to tell her. Apologies he wanted to make.

For the first time since the ordeal began, Cap felt moisture well in his eyes and spill across his cheeks, leaving chill tracks behind.

MACKENNA'S GOLD

WILL HENRY

"Some of the best writing the American West can claim!"

—Brian Garfield, Bestselling Author of *Death Wish*

Somewhere in 100,000 square miles of wilderness is the fabled Lost Canyon of Gold. With his dying breath, an ancient Apache warrior entrusts Glen Mackenna with the location of the lode that will make any man—or woman—rich beyond their wildest dreams. Halfbreed renegade and captive girl, mercenary soldier and thieving scout—brave or beaten, innocent or evil, they'll sell their very souls to possess Mackenna's gold.

_4154-5 $4.50 US/$5.50 CAN

WILL HENRY

WHO RIDES WITH WYATT

"Some of the best writing the American West can claim!"
—*Brian Garfield, Bestselling Author of Death Wish*

They call Tombstone the Sodom in the Sagebrush. It is a town of smoking guns and raw guts, stage stick-ups and cattle runoffs, blazing shotguns and men bleeding in the streets. Then Wyatt Earp comes to town and pins on a badge. Before he leaves Tombstone, the lean, tall man with ice-blue eyes, a thick mustache and a long-barreled Colt becomes a legend, the greatest gunfighter of all time.

BY THE FIVE-TIME WINNER OF THE GOLDEN SPUR AWARD

___4292-4 $3.99 US/$4.99 CAN

WILL HENRY
JOURNEY TO SHILOH

While the bloody War Between the States is ripping the country apart, Buck Burnet can only pray that the fighting will last until he can earn himself a share of the glory. Together with a ragtag band of youths who call themselves the Concho County Comanches, Buck sets out to drive the damn Yankees out of his beloved Confederacy. But the trail from the plains of Texas to the killing fields of Tennessee is full of danger. Buck and his comrades must fight the uncontrollable fury of nature and the unfathomable treachery of men. And when the brave Rebels finally meet up with their army, they must face the greatest challenge of all: a merciless battle against the forces of Grant and Sherman that will truly prove that war is hell.

_4203-7 $4.50 US/$5.50 CAN